Gently Does It

Alan Hunter

ROBINSON

Constable & Robinson Ltd
3 The Lanchesters
162 Fulham Palace Road
London W6 9ER
www.constablerobinson.com

This paperback edition published by Robinson,
an imprint of Constable & Robinson Ltd, 2010

A copy of the British Library Cataloguing in Publication data is available
from the British Library

ISBN: 978-1-84901-498-4

Typeset by TW Typesetting, Plymouth, Devon

Printed and bound in the EU

3 5 7 9 10 8 6 4

For—

ADELAIDE

A GENTLE REMINDER TO THE READER

This is a detective story, but NOT a 'whodunit'. Its aim is to give a picture of a police investigator slowly building up his knowledge of a crime to a point, not where he knows who did it – both you and he know that at a fairly early stage – but to a point where he can bring a charge which will convince the jury.

I thought it worthwhile mentioning this. I hate being criticized for not doing what I had no intention of doing.

Sincerely yours,

ALAN HUNTER

CHAPTER ONE

CHIEF INSPECTOR GENTLY, Central Office, CID, reached automatically into his pocket for another peppermint cream and fed it unconsciously into his mouth. Then he folded his large hands one over the other on the guard rail and peered into the inferno below him with a pleased expression, rather like a middle-aged god inspecting a new annex for the damned.

It was something new in Walls of Death. It was wider, and faster. The young man in red leather overalls was not finding it at all easy to make the grade. He was still tearing madly round the cambered bottom of his cage, like a noisy and demented squirrel, trying to squeeze yet more speed out of his vermilion machine. Chief Inspector Gently watched him approvingly. He had always been a Wall of Death fan. He breathed the uprising exhaust fumes with the contented nostrils of a connoisseur, and felt in his pocket for yet one more peppermint cream.

Suddenly the gyrating unit of man and machine began to slide upwards towards him: a smooth, expert movement, betraying a brain which could judge to a hair. The

1

ear-splitting thunder of a powerful engine in a confined space rose to a crescendo. The solid wooden wall vibrated and swayed threateningly. Higher it crept, and higher, and then, in one supreme gesture, deliberately rehearsed and breathtakingly executed, shot up to the very lip of the guard rail with a roar of irresistible menace and fell away in drunken, flattening spirals.

Chief Inspector Gently smiled benignly at the ducked heads around the guard rail. His jaw continued its momentarily interrupted champing movement. The steadying quality of peppermint creams on the nerves was, he thought, something that deserved to be better known.

Outside the Wall of Death the Easter Fair was in full swing, a gaudy, lusty battleground of noise and music. There were at least five contenders in the musical field, ranging from the monstrous roundabouts that guarded the approach from Castle Paddock to the ancient cake-walk spouting from the cattle-pens, wheezy but indomitable. All of them played different tunes, all of them played without a break. Nobody knew what they were playing, but that was not the point . . .

Chief Inspector Gently shouldered his way tolerantly through the crowd. He didn't like crowds, by and large, but since he was on holiday he felt he could afford to be generous. He stopped at a rock-stall and inspected its brilliant array of starches. 'Have you got any peppermint creams?' he enquired, not very hopefully. They hadn't, so he bought some poisonous-looking bull's-eyes with orange and purple stripes to take back for the landlady's little boy.

A newsboy came thrusting through the crowd, challenging the uproar with leathern lungs. '*Lay-test – lay-test!*

Read abaht the . . .' Gently turned, in the act of putting the bull's-eyes into his pocket. The newsboy was serving a tow-haired young man, a young man still wearing a pair of scarlet leather breeches. Gently surveyed him mildly, noticing the Grecian nose, the blue eyes, the long line of the cheek and the small, neat ears. There was a note of determination about him, he thought. The peculiar quality which Conrad called somewhere 'ability in the abstract'. He would get on, that lad, provided he survived his Wall of Death interlude . . .

And then Gently noticed the long cheek pale beneath its coat of dust and smears of oil. The blue eyes opened wide and the hand that held the paper trembled. The next moment the young man had gone, darted off through the crowd and vanished like a spectre at cockcrow.

Gently frowned and applied to his bag for a peppermint cream. The newsboy came thrusting by with his stentorian wail. 'Gimme one,' said Gently. He glanced over the dry headlines of international conferences and the picture of the film-starlet at Whipsnade: tilted the paper sideways for the stop-press. 'Timber Merchant Found Dead,' he read. 'The body of Nicholas Huysmann, 77, timber merchant, was discovered this afternoon in his house in Queen Street, Norchester. The police are investigating.' And below it: 'Huysmann Death: police suspect foul play.'

For the second time that afternoon the jaw of Chief Inspector Gently momentarily ceased to champ.

Superintendent Walker of the Norchester City Police looked up from a report sheet as Chief Inspector Gently tapped and entered the office. 'Good Lord!' he exclaimed. 'I was just wondering whether we should get on to you. What in the world are you doing down here?'

Gently chose the broader of two chairs and sat down. 'I'm on holiday,' he said laconically.

'On holiday? I didn't think you fellows at the Central Office ever had a holiday.'

Gently smiled quietly. 'I like to fish,' he said. 'I like to sit and watch a float and smoke. I like to have a pint in the local and tell them about the one that got away. They don't let me do it very often, but I'm trying to do it right now.'

'Then you're not interested in a little job we've got down here?'

Gently brought out the battered bag which had contained his peppermint creams and looked into it sadly. 'They'll send you Carruthers if you ask them,' he said.

'But I don't want Carruthers. I want you.'

'Carruthers is a good man.'

Superintendent Walker beat the top of his desk with an ink-stained finger. 'I don't like Carruthers – I don't get on with him. We had a difference of opinion over that Hickman business.'

'He was right, wasn't he?'

'Of course he was right! I've never been able to get on with him since. But look here, Gently, this case looks like being complicated. I've got implicit faith in my own boys, but they don't claim to be homicide experts. And you are. So what about it?'

Gently took out the last of his peppermint creams, screwed up the bag and laid it carefully on the superintendent's desk. The superintendent whisked it impatiently into his waste-paper basket. 'It's this Huysmann affair, is it?' Gently asked.

'Yes. You've seen the papers?'

'Only the stop-press.'

'I've just got a report in from Hansom. He's down there now with the medico and the photographer. Huysmann was stabbed in the back in front of his safe and according to the yard manager there's about forty thousand pounds missing.'

Gently pursed his lips in a soundless whistle. 'That's a lot of money to keep in a safe.'

'But from what we know of Huysmann, it's probably true. He was a naturalized Dutchman who settled down here a good fifty years ago. He's been a big noise in the local timber industry for longer than I can remember and he had an odd sort of reputation. Nothing wrong, you know, just a bit eccentric. He lived a secluded life in a big old house down by the river, near his timber yard, and never mixed with anybody except some of the Dutch skippers who came up with his wood. He married a daughter belonging to one of them, a nice girl called Zetta, but she died in childbirth a few years afterwards. He's got two children, a daughter who lives in the house and is very rarely seen out of it, and a son called Peter, from whom he was estranged. Peter's known to us, by the by – he was the mate of a lorry-driver who got pulled for losing a load of cigarettes. He gave up lorry-driving after that and got a job with a travelling show.'

'He's a Wall of Death rider,' said Gently, almost to himself.

Superintendent Walker's eyebrows rose a few pegs. 'How do you know that?' he enquired.

'Things just sort of pop up on me,' said Gently. 'That's why they stuck me in the Central Office. But don't let it worry you. Keep on with the story.'

The superintendent eyed him suspiciously for a moment, then he leant forward and continued. 'Between you and me, I think Peter is the man we're after. He's here in town with the fair on the cattle market and according to the maid he was at his father's house this afternoon and there was a quarrel. That was just before 4 p.m. and the body was found by the housekeeper at 5 p.m. At least, he was the last person to see Huysmann alive.'

'As far as you know,' added Gently mildly.

'As far as we know,' the superintendent corrected himself. 'The weapon used was one of a pair of Indian throwing knives which hung on the wall. He was stabbed under the left shoulder-blade, the knife penetrating well into the heart. Hansom thinks he was kneeling at the safe at the time and the murderer had to push the body aside to get the money. The money was principally in five-pound and smaller notes.'

'Are any of the numbers known?' enquired Gently.

'We've got a list of numbers from the bank for one hundred of the five-pound notes, but that's all.'

'Who was in the house at the time of the murder?'

'Only the maid, as far as we can make out. The housekeeper had the day off till tea-time: she was out from 11 a.m. till just before five. Gretchen, the daughter, went to the pictures at half-past two and didn't get back till well after five. There's a chauffeur, but he went off duty at midday. The only other person with normal access to the house was the yard manager, who was watching the football match at Railway Road.'

6

Gently pondered a moment. 'I like alibis,' he said, 'they're such fun, especially when you can't disprove them. But this maid, how was it she didn't hear Huysmann being killed? People who're being knifed don't usually keep quiet about it.'

The superintendent twisted his report over and frowned. 'Hansom hasn't said anything about that. He got this report off in a hurry. But I dare say he'll have something to say about it when he's through questioning. The main thing is, are you going to help us out?'

Gently placed four thick fingers and two thick thumbs together and appeared to admire the three-dimensional effect he achieved. 'Did you say the house was by the river?' he enquired absently.

'I did. But what the hell's that got to do with it?'

Gently smiled, slowly, sadly. 'I shall be able to look at it, even if I can't fish in it,' he said.

Queen Street, in which stood the house of Nicholas Huysmann, was probably the oldest street in the city. Incredibly long and gangling, it stretched from the foot of the cattle market hill right out into the residential suburbs, taking in its course breweries, coal-yards, timber-yards, machine-shops and innumerable ancient, rubbishy houses. South of it the land rose steeply to Burgh Street, reached by a network of alleys, an ugly cliff-land of mean rows and wretched yards; northwards lay the river, giving the street a maritime air, making its mark in such nomenclatures as 'Mariner's Lane' and 'Steam Packet Yard'.

The Huysmann house was the solitary residence with any pretension in Queen Street. Amongst the riff-raff of ancient wretchedness and modern rawness it raised its distinguished front with the detached air of an impoverished aristocrat in an alien and repugnant world. At the front it had two gable-ends, a greater and a lesser, connected by a short run of steep roof, beneath which ran a magnificent range of mullioned windows, projecting over the street below. Directly under these, steps rose to the main entrance, a heavily studded black door recessed behind an ogee arch.

Gently paused on the pavement opposite to take it in. A uniformed man stood squarely in the doorway and two of the three cars pulled up there were police cars. The third was a sports car of an expensive make. Gently crossed over and made to climb the steps, but his way was blocked by the policeman.

'No entrance here, sir,' he said.

Gently surveyed him mildly. 'You're new,' he said, 'but you look intelligent. Whose car is ZYX 169?'

The policeman stared at him, baffled. On the one hand Gently looked like an easy-going commercial traveller, on the other there was just enough assurance in his tone to make itself felt. 'I'm afraid I can't answer questions,' he compromised warily.

Gently brought out a virgin, freshly purchased packet of peppermint creams. 'Here,' he said, 'have one of these. They're non-alcoholic. You can eat them on duty. They're very good for sore feet.' And placing a peppermint cream firmly in the constable's hand, he slid neatly past him and through the door.

He found himself in a wide hall with panelled walls and a polished floor. Opposite the door was a finely carved central stairway mounting to a landing, where a narrow

8

window provided the hall with its scanty lighting. There were doors in the far wall on each side of the stairway, two more to the left and one to the right. At the end where he entered stood a hall table and stand, and to the right of the stairway a massive antique chest. There was no other furniture.

As he stood noting his surroundings the door on his right opened and a second constable emerged, followed by a thin, scrawny individual carrying a camera and a folded tripod.

'Hullo, Mayhew,' said Gently to the latter, 'how are crimes with you?'

The scrawny individual pulled up so sharply that the tripod nearly went on without him. 'Inspector Gently!' he exclaimed, 'but you can't have got here already! Why, he isn't properly cold!'

Gently favoured him with a slow smile. 'It's part of a speed-up programme,' he said. 'They're cutting down the time spent on homicide by thirty per cent. Where's Hansom?'

'He – he's in the study, sir – through this door and to the left.'

'Have they moved the body?'

'No, sir. But they're expecting an ambulance.'

Gently brooded a moment. 'Whose is that red sports car parked outside?' he asked.

'It belongs to Mr Leaming, sir,' answered the second constable.

'Who is Mr Leaming?'

'He's Mr Huysmann's manager, sir.'

'Well, find him up and tell him I want to see him, will you? I'll be in the study with Hansom.'

9

The constable saluted smartly and Gently pressed on through the door on the right. It led into a long, dimly lit passage ending in a cul-de-sac, with opposite doors about halfway down. Two transom lights above the doors were all that saved the passage from complete darkness. A heavy, carved chest-of-drawers stood towards the end, on the right. Gently came to a standstill between the two doors and ate a peppermint cream thoughtfully. Then he pulled out a handkerchief and turned the handle of the right-hand door.

The room was a large, well-furnished lounge or sitting-room, with a handsome open fireplace furnished with an iron fire-basket. A tiny window pierced in the outer wall looked out on the street. There was a vase of tulips standing in it. At the end of the room was a very large window with an arched top, but this was glazed with frosted glass. Gently looked down at the well-brushed carpet which covered almost the entire floor, then stooped for a closer inspection. There were two small square marks near the outer edge of the carpet, just by the door, very clearly defined and about thirteen inches apart. He glanced absently round at the furniture, shrugged and closed the door carefully again.

There were five men in the study, plus a sheeted figure that a few hours previously had also been a man. Three of them looked round as Gently entered. The eyes of Inspector Hansom opened wide. He said: 'Heavens – they've got the Yard in already! When the hell are we going to get some homicide on our own?'

Gently shook his head reprovingly. 'I'm only here to gain experience,' he said. 'The super heard I was in town, and he thought it would help me to study your method.'

Hansom made a face. 'Just wait till I'm super,' he said disgustedly, 'you'll be able to cross Norchester right off your operations map.'

Gently smiled and helped himself from a packet of cigarettes that lay at the Inspector's elbow. 'Who did it?' he enquired naïvely.

Hansom grunted. 'I thought you were here to tell me that.'

'Oh, I like to take local advice. It's one of our first principles. What's your impression of the case?'

Hansom seized his cigarettes bitterly, extracted one and returned the packet ostentatiously to his pocket. He lit up and blew a cloud of smoke into the already saturated atmosphere. 'It's too simple,' he said, 'you wouldn't appreciate it. We yokels can only see a thing that sticks out a mile. We aren't as subtle as you blokes in the Central Office.'

'I suppose he was murdered?' enquired Gently with child-like innocence.

For a moment Hansom's eyes blazed at him, then he jerked his thumb at the sheeted figure. 'If you can tell me how an old geezer like that can stab himself where I can't even scratch fleas, I'll give up trying to be a detective and sell spinach for a living.'

Gently moved over to the oak settle on which the figure lay and turned back the sheet. Huysmann's body lay on its back, stripped, looking tiny and inhuman. The jaw was dropped and the pointed face with its wisp of silver beard seemed to be snarling in unutterable rage. Impassively he turned it over. At the spot described so picturesquely by Hansom was a neat, small wound, with a vertical bruise extending about an inch in either direction. Gently covered up the body again.

'Where's the weapon?' he asked.

'We haven't found it yet.'

Gently quizzed him in mild surprise. 'You described it in your report,' he said.

Hansom threw out his hands. 'I thought we'd got it when I made the report, but apparently we hadn't. I didn't know there was a pair. The daughter told me that afterwards.'

'Where's the one you have got?'

Hansom made a sign to the uniformed man standing by. He delved into an attaché case and brought out an object wrapped in cotton cloth. Gently unwrapped it. It was a beautifully ornamented throwing knife with a damascened blade and a serpent carved round the handle. It had a guard of a size and shape to have caused the bruise on Huysmann's back.

'Does it match the wound?' Gently asked.

'Ask the doc,' returned Hansom.

The heavily jowled man who sat scribbling at a table turned his head. 'I've only probed the wound so far,' he said, 'but as far as I can see it's commensurate with having been caused by this or an identical weapon buried to the full extent of the blade.'

'What do you make the time of death?'

The heavily jowled man bit his knuckle. 'Not much later than four o'clock, I'd say.'

'And that's just after your Peter Huysmann was heard quarrelling with his papa,' put in Hansom, with a note of triumph in his voice.

Gently shrugged and walked over to the wall. The room was of the same size as the sitting-room opposite, but differed in having a small outer door at the far side.

Gently opened it and looked out. It gave access to a little walled garden with a tiny summer-house. There was another door in the garden wall.

'That goes to the timber-yard next door,' said Hansom, who had come over beside him. 'We've been over the garden and the summer-house with a fine-tooth comb and it isn't there. I'll have some men in the timber-yard tomorrow.'

'Is there a lock to that door in the wall?'

'Nope.'

'How about this door?'

'Locked up at night.'

Gently came back in and looked along the wall. There was an ornamental bracket at a height of six feet. 'Is that where you found the knife?' he enquired, and on receiving an affirmative, reached up and slid the knife into the bracket. Then he stood there, his hand on the hilt, his eyes wandering dreamily over the room and furnishings. Near at hand, on his right, stood the open safe, a chalked outline slightly towards him representing the position of the body as found. Across the room was the inner door with its transom light. A pierced trefoil window on his left showed part of the summer-house.

He withdrew the knife and handed it back to the constable.

'What has the mastermind deduced?' asked Hansom, with a slight sneer.

Gently fumbled for a peppermint cream. 'Which way did Peter Huysmann leave the house?' he countered mildly.

'Through the garden and the timber-yard.'

'What makes you think that?'

'If he'd gone out through the front door the maid would have known – the old man had a warning bell fitted to it. It sounds in here and in the kitchen.'

'An unusual step,' mused Gently. He turned to the constable. 'I want you to go to the kitchen,' he said. 'I want you to ask the maid if she heard any unusual noise whatever after the quarrel between Peter and his father this afternoon. And please shut all the doors after you. Oh, and Constable – there's an old chest standing by the stairs in the hall. On your way back you might lift the lid and see what they keep in it.'

The constable saluted and went off on his errand.

'We're doing the regular questioning tomorrow,' said Hansom tartly. Gently didn't seem to notice. He stood quite still, with a far-away expression in his eyes, his lips moving in a noiseless chant. Then suddenly his mouth opened wide and the silence was split by such a spine-tingling scream that Hansom jumped nearly a foot and the police doctor jerked his notebook on to the floor.

'What the devil do you think you're doing!' exclaimed Hansom wrathfully.

Gently smiled at him complacently. 'I was being killed,' he said.

'Killed!'

'Stabbed in the back. I think that's how I'd scream, if I were being stabbed in the back . . .'

Hansom glared at him. 'You might warn us when you're going to do that sort of thing!' he snapped.

'Forgive me,' said Gently apologetically.

'Perhaps you break out that way at the Yard, but in the provinces we're not used to it.'

Gently shrugged and moved over to watch the two

finger-print men at work on the safe. Just then the constable burst in.

'Ah!' said Gently. 'Did the maid hear anything?'

The constable shook his head.

'How about you – did you hear anything just now?'

'No sir, but—!'

'Good. And did you remember to look in the old chest by the stairs?'

The impatient constable lifted to the common gaze something he held shrouded holily in a handkerchief. 'That's it, sir!' he exploded. 'It was there – right there in the chest!'

And he revealed the bloodied twin of the knife which had hung on the wall.

'My God!' exclaimed Hansom.

Gently raised his shoulders modestly. 'I'm just lucky,' he murmured, 'things happen to me. That's why they put me in the Central Office, to keep me out of mischief . . .'

CHAPTER TWO

THE TABLEAU IN the study – constable and knife rampant, inspector passive, corpse couchant – was interrupted by the ringing of a concealed bell, followed by the entry of Superintendent Walker. 'We've lost young Huysmann,' he said. 'I'm afraid he's made a break. I should have had him pulled in for questioning right away.'

Hansom gave the cry of a police inspector who sees his prey reft from him. 'He can't be far – he's probably still in the city.'

'He went back to the fair after he'd been here,' continued the superintendent. 'He had tea with his wife in his caravan and did his stunt at 6.15. He was due to do it again at 6.45. I had men there at 6.35, but he'd disappeared. The last person to see him was the mechanic who looks after the machines.'

'He was going to face it out,' struck in Hansom.

'It looks rather like it, but either his nerve went just then or it went when he saw my men. In either case we've lost him for the moment.'

'His nerve went when he saw the paper,' said Gently through a peppermint cream.

16

The superintendent glanced at him sharply. 'How do you know that?' he asked.

Gently swallowed and licked his lips. 'I saw it. I saw him do his stunt. His nerve was certainly intact when he did that.'

'Then for heaven's sake why didn't you grab him?' snapped Hansom.

Gently smiled at him distantly. 'If I'd known you wanted him I might have done, though once he got going he was moving faster than I shall ever move again.'

Hansom snarled disgustedly. The superintendent brooded for a moment. 'I don't think there's much doubt left that he's our man,' he said. 'It looks as though we shan't be needing you after all, Gently. I think we shall be able to pin something on young Huysmann and make it stick.'

'Gently doesn't think so,' broke in Hansom.

'You've come to a different conclusion?' asked the superintendent.

Gently shrugged and shook his head woodenly from side to side. 'I don't know anything yet. I haven't had time.'

'He found the knife for us, sir,' put in the constable defiantly, thrusting it under Walker's nose. The superintendent took it from him and weighed it in his hand. 'Obviously a throwing knife,' he said. 'We've just found out that young Huysmann used to be in a knife-throwing act before he went into the Wall of Death.'

'That's one for the book!' exclaimed Hansom delightedly.

'All in all, I think we've got the makings of a pretty sound case. I'm much obliged to you, Gently, for consenting to help out, but the case has resolved itself pretty simply. I don't suppose you'll be sorry to get back to your fishing.'

Gently poised a peppermint cream on the end of his thumb and inspected it sadly. 'Who was watching Huysmann from the room across the passage this afternoon?' he enquired, revolving his thumb through a half-circle.

The superintendent stared.

'You might print the door handle and the back of the chair that stands just inside,' continued Gently, 'and photograph the marks left on the carpet. Then again,' he turned his thumb back with slow care, 'you might wonder to yourself how the knife came to be in the chest in the hall. I can't help you in the slightest. I'm still wondering myself . . .'

'Well, I'm not!' barked Hansom. 'It's where young Huysmann hid it.'

'Why?' murmured Gently, 'why did he remove the knife at all? Why should he bother when the knife couldn't be traced to him in any way? And if he did, why did he take it into the hall to hide it? Why didn't he take it away with him?'

Hansom gaped at him with his mouth open. The superintendent chipped in: 'Those are interesting points, Gently, and since you've made them we shall certainly follow them up. But I don't think they affect the main issue very materially. We need not complicate a matter when a simple answer is to hand. As it rests, there is no suspicion except in one direction and the suspicion there is very strong. It is our duty to show how strong and to produce young Huysmann to answer it. I do not think it is our duty, or yours, to hunt out side issues that may weaken or confuse our case.'

Gently made the suspicion of a bow and flipped the peppermint cream from his thumb to his mouth. Hansom sneered. The superintendent turned to the constable. 'Fetch the men in with the stretcher,' he said, and when the constable had departed, 'Trencham is going to meet me at the fairground with a search warrant. You'd better come along, Hansom. I'm going to search young Huysmann's caravan.'

Gently said: 'I'm still interested in this case.'

The superintendent paused. He was not too sure of his position. While the matter was doubtful, the sudden appearance of Gently on the scene had seemed providential and he had gratefully enlisted the Chief Inspector's aid, but now that things were straightening out he began to regret it. There seemed to be nothing here that his own men couldn't handle. It was only a matter of time before young Huysmann was picked up: the superintendent was positive in his own mind that he was the man. And the honour and glory of securing a murder conviction was not to be lightly tossed away.

At the same time, he *had* brought Gently into it, and though the official channels had not been used, he was not sure if he had the power to dismiss him out of hand. Neither was he sure if it was policy.

'Stop in if you like,' he said, 'it's up to you.'

Gently nodded. 'It's unofficial. I won't claim pay for it.'

'Will you come along with us to the fairground?'

Gently pursed his lips. 'No,' he said, 'it's Saturday night. I feel tired. I may even go to the pictures . . .'

The constable left in charge was the constable who had found the knife. Gently, who had lingered to see his finger-printing done, called him aside. 'You were present at the preliminary questioning?' he asked.

'Yes, sir. I came down with Inspector Hansom, sir.'

'Which cinema did Miss Huysmann go to?'

'To the Carlton, sir.'

'Ah,' said Gently.

The constable regarded him with shining eyes. 'You'll excuse me, sir, but I would like to know how you knew where the knife was,' he said.

Gently smiled at him comfortably. 'I just guessed, that's all.'

'But you guessed right, sir, first go.'

'That was just my luck. We have to be lucky, to be detectives.'

'Then it wasn't done by – deduction, sir?'

Gently's smile broadened and he felt for his bag of peppermint creams. 'Have one,' he said. 'What's your name?'

'Thank you, sir. It's Letts.'

'Well, Letts, my first guess was that there'd been some post-mortem monkeying because the knife was missing and there was no reason why it should have been. My second guess was that the party who was watching from the other room this afternoon was the party concerned.'

'How did you know the party was watching this afternoon, sir?'

'Because the room was cleaned up before lunch and it was cleaned up today before lunch – witness the tulips with dew on them and the absence of dust. Hence the

20

marks on the carpet were made after lunch. My third guess was that the party concerned was an inside party and not an outside party, and that the odds were in favour of them hiding the knife in the house. Now a person with a bloody knife to hide doesn't waste time being subtle. It could have been in the chest-of-drawers at the end of the passage, but the polished floor in that direction has an unmarked film of dust. The only other easy hiding-place was the chest in the hall. So I guessed that.'

The constable shifted his helmet a fraction and rubbed his head. 'Then it was all guessing after all, sir?' he said slowly.

'All guessing,' Gently reiterated.

'And yet you were right, sir.'

'Which,' said Gently, 'goes to show how much luck you need to be a detective, Letts ... don't forget that when you apply for a transfer.'

'But you've given the case a different look, sir. It could be that somebody else was in this job as well as young Huysmann.'

'Could be,' agreed Gently, 'or it may just mean that somebody's got some pretty virile explaining to do. Remember what the super said, Letts. He was quite right. It's our job to make a case, not to break it. Justice belongs to the court. It's nothing to do with the police.'

The hall, which was gloomy enough by evening light, seemed even gloomier when lit by the low-power chandelier which depended from its high ceiling. As Gently passed through it on his way out a tall figure stepped towards him. Gently paused enquiringly.

'Chief Inspector Gently?'

'That's me.'

'I'm Rod Leaming, Mr Huysmann's manager. They told me you wanted to see me.'

He was a man of about forty, big, dark-haired, dark-eyed, with small well-set ears and features that were boldly handsome. His voice was rounded and pleasant. Gently said: 'Ah yes. You were at the football match. How did the City get on?'

There was a moment's silence, then Leaming said: 'They won, three-one.'

'It was a good match, they tell me.'

Leaming gave a little shrug. 'There were a lot of missed chances. They might have won six-one without being flattered, though of course Cummings was a passenger most of the match. Are you interested in football?'

Gently smiled a far-away smile. 'I watch the Pensioners when I get the chance. Is your car ZYX 169?'

'Yes.'

'It's got mud all over the rear number plate. I thought I'd mention it to you before you were stopped. It's fresh mud.'

'Thanks for the tip. I must have picked it up on the car park this afternoon.'

'It's a clay mud,' mused Gently, 'comes from a river bank, perhaps.'

'The car park at Railway Road lies between the river and the ground.'

'Ah,' said Gently.

Leaming relaxed a little. He pulled out a gold cigarette case and offered it to Gently. Gently took a cigarette. They were hand-made and expensive. Leaming gave him a light and lighted one himself. 'Look,' he said, forcing smoke through his nostrils, 'this is a bad business, Inspector, and it looks pretty black for young Huysmann. But if an outside opinion is any help, I'm one who doesn't think he's the man. I've seen a good deal of Peter at one time or another and he's not the type to do a thing like this.'

Gently blew a neat little smoke-ring.

Leaming continued: 'Of course, I realize there's everything against him. He's been in trouble before and the reason he was estranged from his father is well known.'

'Not to me,' said Gently.

'You haven't heard? But it's bound to come out in the questioning and it's not so very serious. You've got to remember that he was the only son; he was brought up to regard himself as the automatic heir to the business. Well, there's no doubt that Mr Huysmann was a little hard on Peter when it came to pocket money and one day Peter decamped with a hundred pounds or more.'

Gently exhaled a stream of smoke towards the distant chandelier.

'But that was merely youthful high spirits, Inspector. If Peter had had a proper allowance, it would never have happened. It wouldn't have happened then if Peter hadn't fallen in love with an office girl – she's his wife now – and if Mr Huysmann had treated the affair with . . . well, a little more feeling. But there it was, he wouldn't hear of the idea of Peter getting married and though he might have forgiven the embezzlement, he treated the marriage as though it were a personal affront. Poor Peter had a rough time of it after he left home. He wrote to Mr Huysmann on several occasions asking for small sums, but he never received a penny. I'm afraid their relations were very embittered towards the end.'

Leaming paused for comment, but Gently contented himself with another smoke-ring.

'It got so far that Mr Huysmann threatened to cut Peter out of his will and I believe he meant to do it, if he'd had time, though between you and me it would have been a gross injustice. Apart from his temper – and he inherited that from his father – there was nothing vicious in Peter at all. He's a very likeable lad, with a lot of initiative and any amount of guts. He'd have made a very worthy successor in the firm.'

'And you don't think he did it?' queried Gently dreamily.

'I'm positive he didn't! I've known him for ten years and intimately for eight – saw him every day, had him up to spend the evening, often. I'll tell you something more. If you get this lad and try to pin the murder on him, I'll brief the best counsel in England for his defence, cost what it may.'

'It will cost several thousand,' said Gently, helpfully.

Leaming ignored the remark. He breathed smoke through his nose under high pressure. 'I take it that Peter is your guess as well as theirs?' he demanded.

'My guessing is still in the elementary stage.'

'Well, I could see clearly enough what Inspector Hansom thought about it.'

'Inspector Hansom is a simple soul.'

Leaming's powerful brown eyes sought out Gently's absent green ones. 'Then you don't think he did it – you're on my side in this?'

Gently's smile was as distant as the pyramids. 'I'm not on anybody's side,' he said, 'I'm just here on holiday.'

'But you're assisting on the case? Look here, Inspector, I've been thinking this thing over. There's one thing that's going to tell a lot in Peter's favour. It's the money.'

Gently nodded one of his slow mandarin nods.

'There was forty-two thousand pounds in that safe, more or less, and they won't find it with Peter.'

'Why?' asked Gently brightly.

'Why? Because he didn't do the murder, that's why. And as soon as some of those notes that are listed start turning up, it'll be proof positive that the real murderer is still at large.'

Gently surveyed the burnt-down stub of his cigarette thoughtfully, moved over to the chest and stubbed it against the massive iron clasp. Then he raised the lid and dropped the end inside. 'It might work out if the murderer started on the right side of the forty-two thousand,' he said, 'but then again, he might start in the middle . . .' And he let the lid fall back with a bang.

Leaming stood, feet apart, watching him closely. 'At least it's a good lead,' he said.

Gently sighed. 'Police work is full of leads. It's the tragedy of routine . . . and ninety-nine per cent of them lead nowhere.' He came back from the chest. 'If you're going back to the city I could use a lift,' he said.

Leaming dropped him off at Castle Paddock. Gently shambled away, head bent, following the crescent wall at the foot of the Castle Hill, the patriarchal features of the Norman keep silent and peaceful in the dark sky above. From the other side of the Hill rose the glow and the feverish cacophony of the fair. Clark, the owner of the Wall of Death, had tempted back one of his ex-riders. The Greatest Show on Earth continued to do business . . .

In a quieter corner of the fairground Peter Huysmann's young wife stood near the door of her tiny cosmos, biting her lips to keep back tears of humiliation and helplessness. Inside were the policemen. With religious thoroughness they were dismembering and examining her private, familiar things. 'Look,' said a constable, holding up a cheap little necklet that Peter had bought her on her twenty-first birthday, 'wasn't there something like this on the list of stolen properties today?'

Gently came to Orton Place, where a great sunken gap, used as a car park, still offered mute witness of the Baedeker Raids of ten years back. On two sides of the gap blazed the windows of large stores, risen phoenix-wise. But the gap remained a gap. The streets about it were thronged with Saturday-night crowds, gay, noisy, unconscious that somewhere amongst them was a man for whom they were terrible, who feared their slightest glance, who had the mortal horror on him of being seized and dragged to their machine of death. And amongst them too went the hunters, the takers, the accusers, those to whom the killing of Peter Huysmann meant preferment. But they were unconscious of this as of the gap. Habit had staled them both. And after all, *someone* had done for old Huysmann . . . hadn't they?

'Pink!' cried an old man, as Gently drew near him, 'don't forget your pink!' Gently fumbled in his pocket for coppers. 'They did well today,' said the old man. 'Did you see the match, sir?' 'No,' said Gently. He took the paper. 'Isn't there a home match next week too?' he enquired. 'We've got the Cobblers coming, sir – it'll be a good match.' Gently nodded vaguely. 'I may see it,' he said. As he walked on he unfolded the paper and glanced over the headlines. They ran:

MISSED CHANCES AT RAILWAY ROAD
City not flattered by margin
First-half injury to Cummings

Gently pursed his lips, folded the paper and put it carefully away in his pocket.

CHAPTER THREE

I T WAS RAINING.

A generous stream of water escaped from a blocked gutter two stories higher and battered insistently on the zinc-shod window-sill of Gently's window. He raised his head, frowning. Waking up to rain filled him with a sort of hopelessness, a feeling that here was a day to be got over and dismissed as quickly as possible, a day when all normal business ought to be postponed. He blinked and reached out for the cup of tea that should have been there.

Down below in the little dining-room Gently was the only guest at breakfast. It was Sunday, of course . . . for the rest of the world. But there was a fire and a sheaf of Sunday papers, and the breakfast was a fairly lavish plate of bacon, egg, tomatoes and fried bread. Gently turned over a paper as he ate. The Huysmann business hadn't built up yet, there was only a short paragraph headed: TIMBER MERCHANT STABBED TO DEATH. He sifted it with a practised eye to see if his name was mentioned. It wasn't.

Feeling fuller and better, Gently donned his raincoat and sallied forth. The rain was pelting down out of a low, monotonous sky and the streets were practically empty.

In front of the pathetically gay awnings of the provision market a gang of men were shovelling bruised and rotten fruit into a lorry. Behind them rose the pale pastelled mass of the City Hall with its dim portico and slender naked tower. Gently plodded on through the city centre to the castle and the cattle market.

There was something ominous about the deserted fairground. The booths which had yesterday been wells of colour and bright lights were now blinded with screens of old canvas, taut with the rain and flapping dismally. The avenues of alleys between them had ceased to be channels of raucous delight, showed the black, cross-grooved tiles of the cattle market, threatening the ephemerality of usurping pleasure. Gently made his way to the Wall of Death. At the back was a lean-to with one side canvas. He pushed up the flap and went in.

Inside was a bench on which stood one of the red-painted motorcyles, its engine in the process of being stripped down, while another machine leaned against the end of the lean-to. Across from the flap was the entrance to the well, with the ramp up which the riders went. From this came tinkering sounds. Gently went through. Between the cambered bottom and the outer wall a man was crouched, tightening down the bolt which secured a strengthening strut. He looked at Gently suspiciously. Gently shrugged, leaned against the wall, took out his pipe and began to fill it.

Having locked the bolt with wire the man came out. He was short and stuggy, and his brown, porous face looked as though it had been squeezed up in a pair of nutcrackers. He rolled a cigarette, peering at Gently sharply as he licked it.

'Police?' he asked.

Gently transferred the flame of his lighter from his pipe to the stuggy man's cigarette. 'CID,' he said casually. The stuggy man's hand trembled and he drew at the cigarette powerfully.

'Your outfit?' enquired Gently.

'You know it is.'

'You must be Mr Clark.'

'Who'd you think I was – Nye Bevan?'

Gently shook his head seriously. 'Why did Peter go to see his father yesterday afternoon?' he asked, then leaned back against the wall again to give the stuggy man time to think it over.

There was a pause of quite some moments. The stuggy man puffed at his cigarette with industrious energy, flicking it nervously at the end of each puff. Gently drew in smoke with slow deliberateness. There was a ratio of about three to one. At last the stuggy man said: 'S'pose he just went to say "hullo" to his old man.'

Gently removed his pipe. 'No,' he said, and put his pipe back.

The stuggy man's cigarette nearly burst into flames. He said: 'I don't have to tell you anything!'

Gently nodded indefinitely.

'You can't do nofink to me if I keep my trap shut. Why can't you leave us alone? I told them all they wanted to know last night!'

'You didn't tell them what I want to know.'

'Well, haven't you got enough against him, without looking for any more?'

Gently turned over his pipe and let the top ash fall into a little pool of water gathering on the floor. He surveyed the stuggy man with distant green eyes. 'There's a very good case to be made against Peter Huysmann,' he said. 'If he's guilty, the less that's found out the better. But if he's innocent, then everybody concerned had best tell what they know. But perhaps you think he's guilty?'

'Naow!' The stuggy man flipped ash in a wide arc. 'Pete never did a thing like that. You don't know Pete.' He faced Gently fiercely.

'Then the best way you can help him is to answer my question.'

The stuggy man threw down his cigarette-end and ground it to pulp beneath his foot. 'I know you!' he burst out, 'I know you and your questions! It's all very well now, but when it gets to court it will all be twisted against him. I seen it happen before. I seen the way they went to work to hang old George Cooper. All very nice they were, as nice as pie – they only wanted to help him! But what happened when they gits him in court? Every mortal thing what people had told them was used against him – every mortal thing.'

He broke off, breathing heavily through his flattened nose. 'So don't come telling me how I can help him, mister,' he concluded. 'I wasn't born yesterday, d'ye see?'

The growing pool of water on the floor made a sudden dart forward at a sunken tile. Gently moved his foot to higher ground. 'Let's put it another way,' he said smoothly. 'There's a sufficiently sound case against Peter Huysmann to put him in dock and probably hang him. Any further evidence will simply reinforce the case. So it might be good policy to please the police rather than tease them . . . isn't that sense?'

The stuggy man's eyes blazed. 'You haven't got nofink against me, mister!' he exclaimed.

31

'I'm not suggesting we have. Though we might have, some day . . . it's worth remembering.'

'They was at me last night that way – says they might find the Wall was dangerous. But I know where I stand. It isn't no more dangerous here than it was at Lincoln or Newark, nor anywheres else. And I told them so.' He spat into the pool of water.

Gently sighed, and mentally cursed the large feet of Inspector Hansom, whose prints were so painfully visible. The stuggy man produced his tin of tobacco again and began the nervous concoction of a fresh cigarette. Gently lit it for him absently. The rain continued to fall.

'I saw him ride yesterday,' said Gently, apropos of nothing. 'He's a good rider.'

'He's the best man on the Wall in England,' jerked the stuggy man.

'You wouldn't want to lose him.'

'I shan't, if I can help it.'

'If he gets off he'll inherit his father's business.'

The stuggy man shot him a guarded glance, but said nothing.

'Unless he's been cut off, of course,' added Gently. 'I'm told his father intended to make a fresh will.'

The stuggy man drew in an enormous lungful of smoke and jetted it out towards the canvas flap.

'It could be he went to see him about that,' continued Gently, 'and then, in the course of the quarrel that followed—'

'Naow!' broke in the stuggy man.

'Why not?' queried Gently. 'It's the line that logically suggests itself . . .'

'He didn't go about no will!'

32

'You'll have a hard time convincing the City Police that he didn't. It's the obvious reason, and the obvious reason, right or wrong, is peculiarly acceptable to juries.'

'But I tell you he never, mister – he knew all along that the old man was going to cut him out!'

'Then,' said Gently, sighting his pipe at the stuggy man's heart, 'why did he go?'

The stuggy man gulped. 'I offered him halves in the Wall,' he said. 'He reckoned the old man would put up five hundred to be rid of him.'

'Ah,' said Gently dreamily, 'how you make us work for it – how you do!'

He knocked out his pipe and moved over to the canvas flap. The world outside had an arrested, gone-away look, dull and washed out, a wet Sunday. Instinctively, you would be indoors, preferably with a fire. Gently hovered at the flap a moment. He turned back to the stuggy man.

'Where's Peter Huysmann now?' he asked.

'Where you won't bloody well find him!'

Gently shrugged reprovingly. 'I was only asking a civil question,' he said.

Huysmann's caravan was small and cheap, but it had been recently re-painted in a dashing orange and blue: neatly too. Some time and pains had been lavished on it. It stood somewhat apart from its neighbours, beside a plane tree. One entered by steps and a door at the side. Gently knocked.

'Who is it?' called a voice, subdued, coming with an effort.

'A friend,' replied Gently cheerfully.

33

There was movement inside the van. The door was pulled inwards. A young woman of twenty-three or -four stood framed in the tiny passageway. She was brown-haired with blue-grey eyes and round, attractive features. She had a firm, natural figure. She wore an overall. There was a frightened look in her eyes and her mouth was held small and tight. She said: 'Oh – what is it you want?'

Gently smiled reassuringly. 'I've come to be a nuisance,' he said. 'May I come in?'

She stepped back with a sort of hopeless submission, indicating a door to the left of the passage. Gently inserted his bulky figure with care, pausing to wipe his feet on the small rectangle of coconut-matting. It was a minute sitting-room which at night became a bedroom and at mealtimes was a dining-room. In the centre was a boat-type mahogany table, narrow, with wide, folded-down leaves, on which was a bowl of daffodils. There were three windows with flowered print curtains. A settee built along the wall on the right unfolded into a double bed and opposite it, on the other wall, was a cupboard with drawers, on which stood a row of Penguins and cheap editions of novels. Facing the door hung a framed photograph of Peter in an open-necked shirt.

Gently chose a small wooden chair and sat down. 'I'm Chief Inspector Gently of the Central Office, CID,' he said, 'but don't take too much notice of it. I don't cut much ice in these parts.' He looked around him approvingly. 'I've often thought of buying a caravan like this when I retire,' he added.

Mrs Huysmann moved across behind the table and sat down on the settee. She held herself very stiffly and upright. Her eyes never wandered from Gently's face. She said nothing.

Gently glanced at the photograph of Peter. 'How old is your husband?' he enquired.

'Twenty-nine, in August.' She had a soft, low voice, but it was taut and toneless.

'I've only met him once – if you can call seeing him ride meeting him. I liked his riding. It takes real guts and judgment to do that little trick of his.'

'You've seen him ride?' For a moment she was surprised.

'I was here yesterday. I'm on holiday, you know, but they roped me in on this business. I believe they're sorry they did now. I'm so hard to convince. But there you are . . .' He raised his shoulders deprecatingly.

She said: 'You want to ask me something.' It was between a question and a bare statement of fact, colourless, something to be said.

'Yes,' Gently said, 'but don't rush it. I know how painful it is.'

She looked down, away from him. 'They took my statement last night,' she said.

There was a moment during which the rain beat remotely on the felted roof, an ominous moment, razor-sharp: and then tears began to trickle down the tight, mask-like face. Gently looked away. She was not sobbing. The tears came from deeper, from the very depths of humiliation and fear and helplessness. She said: 'I can't tell you anything – I don't know anything . . . they took it all down last night.'

Gently said: 'They had to do it, you know. I've got to do it, too. Otherwise there may be an injustice.'

'He didn't do it – not Peter – not Peter!' she said, and sank forward with a great sigh, as though to say that had drained away the stiffness in her body. She was sobbing now, blindly, a foolish little lace handkerchief crumpled up in a ball between her hands, the shock and the pent-up horror of the night finding outlet at last. Gently moved across and patted her shoulder paternally. He said: 'Cry away now, like a good girl, and when you've finished I'm going to tell you a secret.'

She looked up at him wonderingly, eyes glazed with tears. He went on: 'I oughtn't to tell you this – I oughtn't even to tell myself. But I'm a very bad detective, and I'm always doing what they tell you not to in police college.'

He moved away to the other side of the caravan and began looking at the books. She followed him with her eyes. There was something in his manner that struck through the bitter confusion possessing her, something that gave her pause. She choked into the handkerchief. 'I'm – I'm sorry!' she faltered.

Gently took down a book. 'You've got *Mornings in Mexico*,' he said absently. 'I read an extract from it somewhere. Can I borrow it?'

'It's – Peter's.'

'Oh, I'll let you have it back. There's nothing at my rooms except a telephone directory, and I've read that.'

He came back and sat down beside her. She sniffed and tried to smile. 'I didn't mean to cry,' she said. 'I'm terribly sorry.' Gently produced his bag of peppermint creams and proffered them to her. 'You'll like these – I've been eating them off and on for twenty years. You try one.' He took one himself, and laid the bag open on the end of the table.

'Now,' he said, 'my secret. But first, you can keep a secret, can't you?'

She nodded, chewing her peppermint cream.

'It's this. I, Chief Inspector Gently, Central Office, CID, am morally certain that Peter didn't murder his father. What do you think of that?'

Her eyes widened. 'But—!' she exclaimed.

Gently held up his hand. 'Oh, I know, and you mustn't tell anybody at all. It's a terrible thing for a Chief Inspector to prejudice himself in the early stages of an investigation. I've had to tick people off about it myself. And to tell it to somebody concerned in the case is flat misdemeanour.' Gently paused to fortify himself with another peppermint cream. 'I've been a policeman too long,' he concluded, 'it's high time they retired me. Some day, I might do something quite unforgivable.'

Mrs Huysmann was still staring at him disbelievingly. 'You – you *know* he didn't do it!' she cried.

'No,' said Gently, 'I don't know it. Not yet.'

'But you said—!'

'I said I was morally certain, my dear, which isn't quite the same thing.'

She relapsed slowly into her former forlorn posture. 'Then they'll still charge him with it,' she said.

Gently nodded. 'My moral certainties won't prevent that. Peter's still in grave danger and unless I can produce some hard, irreducible facts pointing in another direction, he may find his innocence very difficult to establish. Which is why I'm here this morning.'

'But I don't know anything – I can't help you at all!'

Gently smiled at a point beyond the blue horizon.

'That is something, my dear, which we will now attempt to discover,' he said.

The rain had washed out any lurking quaintness there might have been in Queen Street. The raw brick tower of the new brewery seemed rawer, the stale flint-and-brick tower of the old breweries staler, the mouldering plaster-and-lath miserable to disintegration. Gently splashed through puddles formed in hollows of the pavement. He stopped to look at a horse-meat shop. Painted a virulent red, it had crudely drawn upon it the faces of a cat and a dog, with the legend: 'Buy our dinners here'. Up the middle of Queen Street rode a lonely sodden figure, a bundle of papers covered by a sack in the carrier of his bicycle. Behind him limped a dog, head down, tail down. At the horse-meat shop the dog raised its head and gave a low whine. But it continued to limp after its master.

Today there were only two cars outside the Huysmann house, a police car and Leaming's red Pashley. The constable on the door saluted smartly. 'Inspector Hansom is in the sitting-room, sir,' he said. Gently disrobed himself of his raincoat and left it hung dripping on the hall-stand. A second constable opened the sitting-room door for him. Inside sat Inspector Hansom at a table, smoking a cigar. Beside him sat a uniformed man with a shorthand notebook.

'Ah!' cried Hansom, 'the Yard itself! We'll have to forget about the third degree after all, Jackson.'

Gently smiled moistly, took out his pipe and began to fill it. 'Forgive me for being late,' he said.

Hansom spewed forth cigar-smoke. 'Don't mention it,' he said, 'we can accommodate ourselves to Metropolitan hours. Just sit down and make yourself at home. There'll be tea and biscuits in half an hour.'

Gently lit his pipe and sat down.

'I suppose you didn't look in at the office this morning,' continued Hansom, a glint in his eye.

'No. Should I have done?'

'It might be an idea, if you want to keep abreast of this case.'

Gently patted the ash down in his pipe with an experienced finger. 'You mean the five-pound note you found in a drawer in Peter Huysmann's caravan, don't you?' he enquired thoughtfully.

'You were at the office then?' demanded Hansom, a little clashed.

'No. But I was at the caravan this morning.'

'Then perhaps you don't know that it was one of the notes taken from Huysmann's safe?'

Gently shrugged. 'Why else would you have taken it away?'

Hansom's eyes gleamed triumphantly. 'And how do you propose to explain that one, Chief Inspector Gently?' he demanded.

Gently patted away at his pipe till the ash was perfectly level, then dusted off his finger on his trousers. 'I don't explain anything,' he said. 'I'm a policeman. I ask questions.'

'It'll take a lot of questions to make this look silly.'

'I should ask myself,' proceeded Gently, 'why Peter left a note there at all, just one. And I should ask myself whether it was likely to be one of those on your list – he had so many others.' He paused.

'And is that all you'd ask?' enquired Hansom with a sneer.

39

'And I think,' added Gently, 'I'd ask Mrs Huysmann if she knew how it came to be there.'

Hansom sat up straight, his cigar lifting. 'So you would, would you?' he said.

'I think I would. Very nicely, of course, so I didn't make her feel she was being kicked in the teeth by a size fifteen boot.'

'Har, har,' said Hansom, 'give me time to laugh.'

'And I should find out that Peter never had but that one note and brought it back with him yesterday in a seething temper and put it in the drawer with express instructions that it wasn't to be touched. Of course, it's technically possible that he had his pocket picked of the balance . . . perhaps that's why he was so angry.'

Hansom snarled: 'And you believe that bosh?'

'I don't believe anything,' said Gently mildly. 'I just ask questions . . .'

The ash dropped off Hansom's cigar and fell neatly on to the blotter in front of him. He grabbed it away savagely. 'See here,' he snapped, 'I know you're dead against us. I know you'd go to any lengths to get young Huysmann off, even though you're as sure as we are that he did it. Because why? Because you're the Yard and you think you've got to show us we're a lot of flat-footed yokels. That's why! That's why you're going to upset this case – if you can. But you can't, Chief Inspector Gently, it's getting much too one-sided, even for you. By the time we've lined this case up there won't be a jury in the country who'll give it more than ten minutes – if they give it that!'

Gently leaned back in his chair and blew the smallest and roundest of smoke-rings at the distant ceiling. 'Inspector Hansom,' he said, 'I'd like to make a point.'

'What's that?' snarled Hansom.

'There is between us, Inspector Hansom, a slight but operative difference in rank. And now, if you will start sending these people in, we'll try to question them as though we were part of one of the acknowledged civilizations.'

CHAPTER FOUR

M RS TURNER, THE housekeeper, was a clean,
neat, bustling person of fifty-five, dressed for the
day in a black tailored suit smelling of stale lavender. She
had a large bland face with small mean eyes, and her nose
was the merest shade red.

She said: 'I'm sure there's nothing more I can tell you
what I didn't say yesterday,' and sat down with an air of
disapproval and injury.

Hansom said: 'You are Mrs Charles Turner, widow,
housekeeper to the deceased. You had the day off
yesterday till 5 p.m . . . where did you spend the day?'

'I told you all that yesterday.'

'Please be good enough to answer the question. Where
did you spend the day?'

'I went to see me sister at Earlton . . .'

'You were at your sister's the whole of that time?'
Gently said.

The housekeeper shot him a mean look. 'Well, most
of it, like . . .'

'You mean that part of the time you were somewhere
else.'

She pursed her lips and jiffled a little. 'I spent the day with me sister,' she repeated defensively, adding, 'you can ask her, if you don't believe me.'

'Right. We'll check on that,' said Hansom. 'What time did you arrive back here?'

'I got in about five to five.'

'What did you do then?'

'I went into the kitchen to see if the maid had got things ready for tea.'

'You found the maid in the kitchen?'

'She was sitting down reading one of them fourpenny novels.'

'Did she mention anything unusual that had occurred during the afternoon?'

'She said as how Mr Peter had called and seen his father, and they'd had a dust-up over something, but it didn't last long.'

Gently said: 'She could not have heard them quarrelling from the kitchen. Did she say where she was at the time?'

The housekeeper frowned. She didn't like Gently's questions. He seemed determined to complicate the most clear-cut issues. 'I didn't ask her,' she replied tartly.

Hansom continued: 'When did you go to the study?'

'I went there straight away, to ask Mr Huysmann what time he wanted tea.'

'Was that usual?' chipped in Gently.

'Yes, it was usual! He didn't have no set times for his meals. You had to go and ask him.'

'That would be a few minutes after 5 p.m.?' proceeded Hansom.

'About five-past, I should think.'

'And you knocked on the door and entered?'

'That was how he told us to go in.'

'Tell us what you saw when you entered.'

'Well, I just see Mr Huysmann lying there sort of twisted like, as though he might have had a fit.'

'Was he lying in the same position as he was when the police arrived?'

'I might have moved him a little bit, but not much. I thought as how he was took ill. I tried to get him up, but when I saw all the blood under him I knew that something horrible had happened, so I put him back again.'

'And then?'

'Then I went for Susan and told her to get the police.'

'Did Susan go into the study?'

'No, I told her not to. That was bad enough for me, who've seen dead people. I nearly went out when I got back to the kitchen.'

'A telephone message was received at headquarters at 5.17 p.m. That was ten minutes after you would have returned to the kitchen.'

'Well, there I was in a bad way, I had Susan fetch me some brandy. And then Miss Gretchen, she came back and had to be told.'

'What time did Miss Huysmann return?'

'About a quarter past five, I suppose it was.'

'At which door did she enter?'

'She came in the front, of course. Susan was just going through to phone and she see Miss Gretchen in the hall and tell her.'

'How did Miss Huysmann take the news?'

'Well, she's always a very quiet sort of girl, but she was

44

mortal pale when she came into the kitchen. I gave her a sip of brandy to pull her together.'

'Was Susan at all surprised when Miss Huysmann came in?'

'She said: "Oh – I thought you was still in your room, miss."'

Hansom paused, leaned back in his chair and appeared to be studying the rash his cigar-ash had made on his blotter. The constable beside him scribbled industriously. Outside the rain made a soft quiet noise, like the sound of time itself. The housekeeper sat upright and rocked very gently backwards and forwards.

Hansom said: 'You have been a long time in this family, Mrs Turner. Certain private matters concerning it must have come to your notice. Can you think of anything which may have a bearing on the present tragedy?'

The housekeeper's face changed to defensive righteousness. 'There's Mr Peter,' she said, '*he's* no secret.'

'Is there anybody else connected with Mr Huysmann who, to your knowledge, may have had a grudge against him?'

'I daresay there's several people as weren't over-fond of him. He was a long way from being open-handed. But I can't think of anybody who'd want to do a thing like this.'

'Did you know that Mr Huysmann proposed to make a fresh will disinheriting his son?'

'Oh yes. He'd been talking about that ever since Mr Peter got married.'

Gently said: 'How long ago was that?'

The housekeeper thought for a moment. 'It'll be just on two years,' she replied.

'Did Peter know about it two years ago?'

'Mr Huysmann told him before he got married.'

Gently nodded his slow, complacent nod. Hansom glared across at him. 'Is there anything else you'd like to ask before we let Mrs Turner go?' he asked bitingly.

Gently placed his fingers neatly together. 'Was the safe door open or closed when you discovered the body?' he said.

'It was open.'

'And how about the outer door?'

'I think it was closed.'

'Ah,' said Gently. He leaned forward in his chair. 'At the time the murder was discovered, are you positive that Susan and yourself were the only persons in the house?' he asked.

The housekeeper's face registered surprise followed by indignation. 'If there had been anyone else I should have said so,' she retorted magnificently.

'Is there anybody not so far mentioned whom you would not have been surprised to find in the house at that time in the afternoon?'

She paused. 'Well, there's the chauffeur, but he was off duty. And there might have been someone from the yard about business.'

Gently nodded again and rested his chin on his thumbs. 'This room we're in,' he said, 'was it last cleaned before lunch yesterday?'

'You'd best ask Susan about that. It should have been done.'

'To your knowledge, did anybody enter it after the discovery of the murder?'

'There was nothing to come in here about.'

Gently leant far back into his chair, elevated his paired fingers and looked through them at the ceiling. 'During the time when you were not at your sister's yesterday,' he said, 'would you have been . . . somewhere else . . . for the purpose of taking alcoholic refreshment?'

The housekeeper's face turned scarlet. She jumped to her feet, her eyes flashing, and seemed on the point of a scathing denial. Then, with an effort, she checked herself and flung out of the room like an outraged duchess.

Gently smiled through the cage of his fingers. 'Pass me,' he said dreamily, 'there's one alibi less on my list.'

Gently was eating a peppermint cream when Susan came in. He had offered one to Hansom as a sort of olive branch, but Hansom had refused it, and after counting those that remained in the bag Gently was not sorry. He had a feeling that Norchester would not be very productive of peppermint creams on a Sunday, especially a wet Sunday, and the prospect of running short was a bleak one. Life was hard enough without a shortage of peppermint creams.

Susan was a pretty, pert blonde girl with a tilted bra and an accentuated behind. She wore a smile as a natural part of her equipment. She had a snub nose and dimples and a pleased expression, and had a general supercharged look, as though she was liable to burst out of her black dress and stockings into a fierce nudity.

The constable with the shorthand notebook sighed as she took her seat. He was a young man. Hansom ran through the preliminaries of identification and association.

'What time did the family finish lunch, Miss Stibbons?' he asked.

Susan leant her bewitching head on one side. 'It would be about two o'clock, Inspector. It was quarter past when I went to clear away.'

'Did Mr Huysmann go to his study directly after lunch?'

'I wouldn't know, Inspector. But he was there when I took him his coffee.'

'When was that?'

'It would be about half-past two, I should think.'

'What was he doing then?'

'He was standing by the window, looking at the garden.'

'Did he make any remark out of the ordinary?'

The bewitching head dipped over an errant blush. 'We-ell, Inspector . . .'

'Did he lead you to suppose he was expecting a visitor?'

'No . . . he didn't give me that impression.'

Hansom looked her over thoughtfully. He was only forty himself. 'What did Miss Huysmann do after lunch?' he asked.

'She took her coffee up to her room.'

'She apparently left the house shortly afterwards to go to the pictures. She says she left at half-past two. You didn't see her go?'

'No, Inspector.'

'Did she take her coffee to her room before you took Mr Huysmann's to him?'

'Oh yes, she came and got it from the kitchen.'

'You didn't hear the front-door bell between the time she took her coffee and the time you went to the study with Mr Huysmann's?'

'No, Inspector.'

'Nor while you were in the study?'

'No, I didn't hear it at all till Mr Peter came.'

'Because of that you were surprised to find that she had, in fact, gone out?'

'It surprised me at the time, Inspector, but after I'd thought about it I realized she must have gone out through the kitchen.'

'Why should she have done that?'

'We-ell, I don't think she would want her father to know she had gone to the pictures.'

Gently broke in: 'Was it unusual for Miss Huysmann to go to the pictures?'

Susan embraced him in a smile of melting intensity. 'Mr Huysmann didn't think it proper for girls to go to them. But she went when Mr Huysmann was away on business and sometimes she pretended to go to bed early and I would let her out by the kitchen.'

'Wasn't it unusual for her to slip out in the afternoon, when her father might enquire after her?'

'Ye-es . . . she'd never done that before.'

'You have no doubt that she did go out?'

'Oh no! I saw her come in with her hat and coat on.'

'You heard nothing during the afternoon to suggest that she might still be in the house?'

'Nothing at all.'

'Miss Huysmann deceived her father over the matter of the pictures. Do you know of any other way she may have deceived him?'

Susan placed a smooth, conical finger on her dimpled chin and appeared to consider deeply. 'He was very strict,' she said at last.

'You haven't answered the question, Miss Stibbons.'

Susan came back with her take-me smile. 'We-ell, she used to read love-stories and other books that Mr Huysmann didn't know about . . .'

Gently shrugged and extended an open palm towards Hansom. In his mind's eye the figure of the deceased timber-merchant began to take form and substance. He saw the foxy, snarling little face, the sharp, suspicious eyes, the spare figure, the raging, implacable temper of a small man with power . . . the man whose son had kicked free at any price, whose daughter was in league with the maid to deceive him: who declared the cinema improper while he ruffled Susan in his study . . . An alien little man, who had spent most of his life in a new country without making friends, shrewd, sudden, tyrannical and hypo-critical . . .

Hansom continued with the questioning. 'What did you do after you had taken Mr Huysmann his coffee?'

'I cleared away the lunch things and washed up, Inspector.'

'What time would that be?'

'I couldn't say, exactly. I finished washing up about quarter past three, because there was a change of programme on the wireless just then.'

'What programme was that?'

'It was a football match.'

'At what time did it finish?'

'It was just before four, I think.'

'Who won?' put in Gently curiously. Susan flashed him another smile. 'The Rovers beat the Albion two-nought,' she said. Hansom snorted.

'Did you hear the whole programme?' he proceeded.

'We-ell, I had to go and let Mr Peter in.'

'What time was that?'

'It was just as the Rovers scored their first goal.'

Hansom drew his fingers wearily across his face. 'And what time would that be, if it isn't too much to ask?'

The constable with the notebook cleared his throat. 'Beg pardon, sir, but the Rovers scored their first goal in the twenty-ninth minute.'

Hansom stared at him.

'If the kick-off was at three, sir, it would make the time exactly 3.29 p.m.'

'Ah,' said Hansom heavily, 'so it would, would it? Thank you very much. Make a note of it. You're a credit to the force, Parsons.'

'I'm a student of soccer, sir,' said Parsons modestly.

'So am I,' said Gently.

Hansom drew a deep breath and looked from one to the other. 'Why don't you get your pools out?' he yapped. 'Who am I to butt in with my homicide? Send out for the papers and let's get down to a session!'

Parsons retired to his notebook, crushed, and Gently took out his peppermint creams.

'Now!' said Hansom, 'you appear to have let in Peter Huysmann at 3.29 p.m. Greenwich. Who did he ask to see?'

'He said he'd come to see his father, Inspector, and asked if he was in.'

'Was there anything unusual in his aspect?'

'He did seem a little off-hand, but Mr Peter is like that sometimes.'

'Did you show him into the study?'

'I told him his father was there, and then I went back to the kitchen.'

'It must have been an exciting match,' said Hansom bitterly. 'What happened then?'

'I got on with washing the salad for tea.'

'How did it come about that you heard Mr Huysmann and his son quarrelling?'

'Well, there wasn't a salad bowl in the kitchen, so I had to fetch one from the dining-room. I heard them at it as I was passing through the hall.'

'Time?'

'I don't really know, Inspector.'

'Nobody scoring any goals?'

'Not just then.'

Hansom rolled his eyes. 'I wonder if I could pin anything on those boys for withholding assistance from the police ... Was it much before the end of the programme?'

'Oh yes ... quite a long time before.'

'Did you go down the passage to listen?'

Susan gave him a well-taken look of sad reproof. 'No, Inspector.'

'Why not? It should have been worth listening to.'

'But there'd been so many of them before.'

'And then, of course, the Albion might have equalized. Did you hear anything at all of what was said?'

'We-ell, I heard Mr Peter say his father hadn't got any human feelings left.'

'And what did Mr Huysmann say?'

'He said something that sounded nasty, but he had a funny way of speaking. You couldn't always understand him.'

'And that was positively all you heard of a quarrel following which Mr Huysmann was stabbed to death?'

Susan frowned prettily and applied her finger to the dimple in her chin again. 'We-ell, when I was coming back from the dining-room I heard Mr Peter say something about he'd take it, but there'd be a time when he'd give it back.'

'Have you any idea to what he was referring?'

'Oh no, Inspector.'

'You didn't,' mused Gently, 'you didn't hear anything to suggest that the object referred to ... *wasn't* ... a five-pound note?'

Susan looked puzzled. 'I don't think so,' she said.

Hansom breathed heavily. 'So you went back to the kitchen,' he said. 'Well – what did you do then?'

'I finished the salad and cut some bread and butter.'

'Did you hear nothing unusual while you were doing that?'

'No, Inspector.'

'Nothing resembling cries or a struggle?'

'You can't hear anything from that side of the house in the kitchen.'

'How about the warning bell on the front door?'

'I didn't hear it ring.'

'After the sports interlude – did you turn the wireless off?'

'Oh no, it was dance music after that. I had it on all the while. It was Mrs Turner who switched it off when she came in.'

'How long did it take you to finish preparing the tea?'

'I'd done by ten past four. After that I made a cup of tea and some toast, and sat down for a bit till Mrs Turner got back at five. It should have been my evening off,' she added glumly.

'What happened when Mrs Turner got back?'

'Well, she took her things off and looked to see if I'd done the tea properly, then she went to ask Mr Huysmann when he'd be wanting it.'

'And then?'

'She came back a minute or two later looking as white as a sheet. "Oh God!" she said, "there's something terrible happened to the master. Don't go near the study," she said. It was awful, Inspector!'

'Mrs Turner sent you for some brandy. Where was it kept?'

'I got the decanter from the dining-room.'

Gently leant forward. 'When you passed through the hall to the dining-room, did you see anybody?' he enquired.

'No, nobody.'

'Did you hear or see anything unusual?'

'I can't remember anything.'

Gently brooded a moment. 'Mrs Turner then sent you to telephone the police. Which telephone did you use?'

'I used the one in the little place under the stairs.'

'As you entered the hall you met Miss Gretchen. Where did you first see her?'

'She was just come in. She was taking her hat off.'

'Was the door open or closed?'

'It was closed.'

'Did you hear the warning bell just before or as you were leaving the kitchen?'

'We-ell . . . I might have done.'

'Can you say for certain that you did?'

Susan bathed him in her dissolving smile. 'Yes,' she said, 'I think I can.'

Gently eased back in his chair and studied illimitable realms of space. 'Do you not think it strange,' he said, 'that Miss Gretchen should re-enter the house by the front door with its warning bell, which she was at such pains to avoid when she went out?'

For a brief second the blue eyes stared at him in complete blankness. Then they swam to life again. 'She'd got an evening paper,' said Susan, 'I dare say she'd have said she went out to buy one.'

'Ah!' breathed Gently, 'an evening paper. That's the second one that's cropped up in this case.' He waved her back to Hansom.

'The Chief Inspector has forgotten to ask you his most telling question,' said Hansom acidly.

Gently inclined his head.

'He wants you to tell him if you entered this room any time after lunch yesterday.'

Susan glanced at Gently in puzzlement.

'Well, go on,' said Hansom, 'tell him.'

Gently said: 'Not after lunch but after you cleaned the room out.'

Susan wrinkled her snow-white brow. 'I put the flowers in the window. I didn't go in after that. I don't think anybody did.'

'You've made him happy,' said Hansom, 'you'll never know how happy you've made the Chief Inspector.' And he laughed in his semi-handsome way.

CHAPTER FIVE

HANSOM WAS SMOKING again: the air was thickening with the fulsome smell of his Corona. Gently, too, was adding smoke-rings to the upper atmosphere. The constable sniffed in a peaked sort of way. 'Go on,' said Hansom, 'be a devil. Have a spit and a draw.' The constable said, 'Thank you, sir,' and fished out a somewhat tatty cigarette. Hansom gave him a light. He said: 'The super doesn't smoke, and he's the one person around here who can afford to.' Gently said: 'You'll have to transfer to the MP and get the London scale.' Hansom grunted.

They could hear the rain still, outside. There was a drain by the pavement just outside the big window which made little, ecstatic noises. To hear that made the room seem chill. 'There's the chauffeur and the manager and Miss Gretchen,' said Hansom. 'Who'd you like to have in next?'

Gently said: 'Was there anyone in the yard yesterday?'

'Nope,' Hansom said. 'Saturday.'

Gently blew a few rings. 'Let's have the chauffeur,' he said. 'He's probably sweating on his pint before lunch.

After him I'd like to see Miss Gretchen. We'll keep Leaming for dessert.'

Hansom called in the constable from outside.

The chauffeur's name was Fisher. He was a tall, broad-shouldered, athletic-looking man of thirty, dark-haired, dark-eyed, with a strong but rather brutal face and lop-ears. He had a small moustache, carefully trimmed. He wore a beach-girl tie and a cheap American-style jacket in two patterns.

Hansom said: 'What time did you go off duty yesterday?'

'About twelve or just after,' Fisher replied slowly. 'I'd just cleaned the car down.' He had a hard but slovenly voice.

'What did you do when you went off duty?'

'I had a beer in the "Lighterman".'

'And after that?'

'Had something to eat in the snack-bar – Charlie's, they call it.'

'What time did you leave the snack-bar?'

'I dunno. Might've been half-past one.'

'Where did you go then?'

'I went back to my place and had a lie-down.'

'Where's your place?'

'5A Paragon Alley. It's up the hill towards Burgh Street. It's a flat.'

'Do you live alone?'

'There's a woman comes in of a morning.'

'Did anybody see you there?'

'I dunno. There may've been someone about, but it's quiet up the Alley.'

'How long were you lying down?'

'Hour, maybe.'

'What did you do then?'

'I got on with my model.'

'What's that?'

Fisher moved his long, sprawling legs. 'I make scale model planes – it's a hobby. I'm making an S.E. 5.'

'How long were you doing that?'

'Till four o'clock.'

Gently said: 'You remember that time very precisely. I wonder why?'

Fisher stirred again, uneasily. 'I just thought I'd work on it till four, that's all. There wasn't any reason. I just thought I'd work on it till four.'

Hansom continued: 'What did you do after four?'

'I went up to the fair.'

'Did you meet anyone you recognized?'

'I saw Mr Peter go across to the Wall from his caravan.'

'Time!' snapped Gently, beating Hansom to it by a fair margin.

Fisher jumped at the suddenness of the question. 'It was twenty-five past four.'

'How do you know?'

'I just looked at my watch.'

'Why?'

'I dunno – I just looked at my watch!'

'Do you often just look at your watch, or is it only when you know you may have to account for your movements?'

'I didn't know anything – I just looked at it!'

Gently paused like a stalking jaguar. Fisher's brow was tight and moistening with perspiration. 'What was he wearing?' purred Gently.

'He was going to the Wall – he'd got his overalls on.'

'You mean the red leather ones he rides in?'

'That's right.'

'And he was going to the Wall?'

'I said he was!'

'Then how do you account for the fact that the overalls are kept at the Wall and not at the caravan?'

'I dunno – perhaps he wasn't coming from the caravan—'

'But you said he was.'

'I thought he was – he was coming from that way—'

'How many things have you thought up to tell us?'

'I haven't thought anything – it's the truth!'

'When did you hear about the murder?'

'They told me when I came in this morning.'

'Who's "they"?'

'Mrs Turner.'

'When did it take place?'

'About four.'

'How do you know?'

'She told me!'

'But Mrs Turner didn't find the body till five. How did she know that the murder took place at four?'

'I dunno – she just told me!'

'And you just happened to be looking at the time and deciding to go out at four?'

'Yes, I did!'

'Would you describe that as being coincidental in any way?'

'I dunno, but it's true!'

Gently swam forward in his chair. 'It's true that you can give no verifiable account of your movements between 1.30 and 4.25 p.m. yesterday. It's true that you know the approximate time at which the murder took place and that Mrs Turner could not have done. And it's true that you've taken care to give your movements precise times at and immediately after the murder took place. All these things,' he added thoughtfully, 'would be equally true of the murderer himself.'

Fisher jumped to his feet. 'But I didn't do it!' he cried, 'I didn't – and you can't say I did! You're asking me all these things and twisting them round to make it seem like I did it, but I didn't, and you can't prove that I did!'

'I haven't suggested that you did,' said Gently smoothly. 'I'm merely establishing that you could, perhaps, be more helpful to this enquiry than in fact you are.'

Fisher stood breathing quickly and staring at him. 'I don't know anything,' he said, a note of sullenness in his voice. 'I've told you what I know, and you can't prove anything else.'

Gently looked from Fisher to the chair on which he had been sitting. 'Your chair,' he said, 'we had it finger-printed last night.'

The chauffeur moved away from it involuntarily.

'Do you think it possible that we shall find your prints on it?'

'You'd find them there now, wouldn't you?'

'But would they have been there last night?'

'They might be there any time. I'm about the house. I move the furniture for them sometimes.'

Gently sighed and extended his palm towards Hansom, who had been following the proceedings very attentively.

Hansom said: 'Were you or were you not in this house at the time of the murder?'

60

'I told you I wasn't.'

'Did you witness the murder by standing on that chair and watching through the transom lights?'

'No! I was nowhere near the place.'

'The answers you have given to Chief Inspector Gently suggest to me very strongly that you had knowledge of the crime prior to this morning. Think carefully, now. Are you sure you've nothing to add to what you've already told us?'

'No, I haven't.'

'You've told us the whole truth?'

'Yes!'

'You wouldn't like to reconsider any part of it?'

'It's the truth, I tell you!'

'And it had bloody well better be, for your sake!' bawled Hansom, suddenly dropping his official mask in exasperation. 'Now get out of here and hold yourself ready for further questioning.'

Fisher flushed angrily and turned towards the door.

'Just a minute,' said Gently. Fisher paused. 'Why did you put it in the chest?' enquired Gently confidentially.

The chauffeur stared at him with complete lack of understanding. 'Put *what* in the chest?' he asked.

Gently swam back into the depths of his chair. 'Never mind,' he said, 'run along. Do what the Inspector tells you . . .'

Hansom blasted the butt of his cigar in the ashtray and took one of his very deepest breaths. He said: 'I've got to hand it to you. I never thought there was much in that hoo-ha about the chair, but I'm beginning to have my doubts.'

'It's just guess-work,' replied Gently deprecatingly. 'The maid might have missed those marks when she brushed the carpet.'

'I'm willing to swear that fellow was in here like you said.'

'There's nothing to prove it, yet. Fisher's got an alibi that'll take a lot of breaking and you've seen what luck I've had trying to establish that there was someone else in the house.'

'He was lying. He was lying himself black in the face. I'll have him down at headquarters and see what I can get out of him there.'

Gently nodded a pensive nod.

'Not that I can see how it'll help young Huysmann,' added Hansom suspiciously. 'If Fisher is shielding him and we make him talk, that'll put the kybosh on you, good and proper.'

Gently smiled agreeably. 'Always supposing that Peter is your man.'

'You know he's our man!' snorted Hansom. 'Good grief, why not admit it? Apart from anything else, who else would want to rub the old man out?'

'Well, there was forty thousand pounds lying about.'

'That's all my eye! That could have been sprung without deliberately knocking him off first. They'd only to wait till he wasn't there. And whoever did it didn't come armed – they did it on impulse, after they got there, after they'd chewed the rag with the old man – which means it was somebody he knew. I tell you, the jury'll be solid.'

Gently's smile grew further and further away. 'There's one thing that puzzles me about our friend Fisher,' he mused.

'And what's that?'

'He didn't seem to me the type who would shield anybody . . . especially with his own neck sticking out as far as it does.'

There was something virginal and nun-like about Gretchen Huysmann, not altogether accounted for by the large silver cross that depended on her bosom. She was not a pretty woman. Her face was pale and a little long, and she wore her straight black hair divided in the middle and caught up in a flat bun. She had small, close-set ears and dark, but not black eyes, now a little reddened and fearful. There was a waxenness about her complexion. She was above medium height. Her figure, which should have been good, was neglected and bundled anyhow into a long, full dress of dark blue. She wore coarse stockings and flat-heeled shoes. She was twenty-seven.

Hansom said: 'Sit down, Miss Huysmann, and make yourself comfortable.' Gretchen sat down, but she did not make herself comfortable. She sat forward on the edge of the chair, her knees together and her feet apart. Her pale face turned from one to another of them quick, frightened glances; her small mouth grew smaller still. She reminded Gently of a plant that had grown in the dark, at once protected and neglected. In this room of three serious men with its alien smell of tobacco smoke she seemed shrunk right back into herself.

Gently motioned to the constable. 'It's getting thick in here. Open that top window.' The constable manipulated the cords that let fall a pane high up in the big window, letting in a nearer sound of rain with a welcome current of new-washed air. Gently beamed encouragingly at Miss Huysmann.

Hansom cleared his throat and said: 'I'd like you to understand, Miss Huysmann, that we fully appreciate the tragic circumstances in which you find yourself. We shall keep you here the shortest possible time and ask you only those questions which it is absolutely necessary for us to have answered.'

Miss Huysmann said: 'I'll . . . tell you all I can to help.' She spoke in a low tone with a slight accent.

Hansom continued: 'Can you remember if your father was expecting any visitors yesterday?'

'I do not know, he would not tell me that.'

'Was it usual for him to receive visitors on a Saturday afternoon?'

'Oh no, practically never. The yard is closed, everyone has gone home.'

'Did you notice anything unusual in his manner at lunch yesterday?'

'I do not think so. He did not speak to me very much at meal-times. Yesterday he said, "Your brother is in town. Take care I do not hear you have been seeing him," but that was all.'

'Were you in the habit of seeing your brother when he was in Norchester?'

'Oh yes, I see him sometimes. But my father, he did not like that.'

'Did you see your brother on this occasion?'

'I see him on the Friday, when I go out to pay some bills.'

'Did he speak of calling on your father?'

'He said he must see him before he leave Norchester.'

'What reason did he give for that?'

'He said that the man for whom he worked had offered him to be partners, but he must have five hundred pounds. So he will ask my father to lend it to him.'

'Did he say lend it?'

'Oh yes, he know my father will not give it to him.'

Hansom toyed with the little pearl-handled penknife that lay on his blotter and glanced towards his cigar case, but Gently clicked disapprovingly. Hansom proceeded:

'What time did lunch finish yesterday?'

'It was about two o'clock.'

'And what did you do after lunch?'

'First, I have a wash. Then I go and fetch my coffee from the kitchen, which I take up to my room. As I am drinking it, I get ready to go out to the pictures.'

Gently said: 'Your visits to the pictures were clandestine, I understand.'

'Pardon?'

'You were obliged to go secretly – your father did not approve.'

Gretchen looked down at the two pale, plump hands twisted together in her lap. 'It is true, I go without his permission. He think the pictures are . . . all bad. And so, I must not go.'

'Did you feel that your father was being severe in forbidding you to go to the pictures?'

'I think, perhaps . . . he did not know how they were. It was safer that I should not go.'

'You thought, at least, that he was being unreasonable.'

'I cannot say. No doubt it was very wrong of me. It may be that this is a judgment, because I do wrong.'

'Did your father ever find out that you had been to the pictures?'

'Once, he caught me.'

'What steps did he take?'

'I was not to leave my room for two days and must not go out of the house for a month.'

'And after that, I take it, you were more cautious?'

The pale hands knotted and pulled apart, but came together again immediately. 'At first, I went only when he was away on business. Then, Susan helped me. I used to pretend I had a headache and go to bed, but I creep downstairs again and out through the kitchen. It was very wrong of me to do this.'

'Miss Huysmann, when you planned to go to the pictures in the afternoon yesterday, you were surely taking an unusual risk?'

'I do not know – my father is usually in the study all the afternoon.'

'But he might easily have asked for you.'

'Oh yes, it could be so. But if Susan came to my room and find me not there, she tell him I am not feeling well, I am lying down and asleep.'

'Following the occasion on which you were caught, had you ever ventured out previously on a Saturday afternoon?'

Her small mouth sealed close. She shook her head forlornly.

'And yet yesterday you did so, without even taking the precaution of first warning Susan. Why was that?'

'I do not know. There is a film I very much want to see . . . all at once, I think I will go.'

'When did you decide that?'

'Oh . . . during lunch.'

'But after lunch you went to the kitchen to fetch your coffee. Why didn't you tell Susan then?'

She shook her head again. 'Perhaps I do not really decide till later, till I take my coffee back to my room.'

'At what time did you leave the house?'

'I think it is twenty-five past two.'

'And you left through the kitchen?'

'It was the only way, if my father is not to know.'

'Why didn't you tell Susan when you passed through on your way out?'

'I do not know . . . perhaps I did tell her.'

'Miss Huysmann, Susan was in the kitchen till half-past two, but she did not see you go out. She was surprised to find that you were out. Yet you claim to have left the house at twenty-five past two.'

Gretchen's dark swollen eyes fixed upon him, pleading and fearful. 'Perhaps it was later when I left . . . perhaps it was after half-past two.'

'How much later?'

'One minute . . . two minutes . . .'

'It was not as late, say, as four-fifteen?'

'Oh no! I was not here, no, no!'

'You were not in the house at all between, say, 2.35 and 5.10?'

'During all that time I was at the pictures.'

'Ah.' Gently sighed, and directed her back to Hansom with an inclination of his head. Hansom picked up the questioning neatly where it had been taken away from him.

'You dressed to go out while you were drinking your coffee. You left the house by the kitchen at a few minutes after 2.30. What did you do then?'

'I went straight to the Carlton cinema.'

'What were they showing there?'

'The big film is called *Scarlet Witness*.'

'Is that what was showing when you entered the cinema?'

'Oh yes, but I came in at the end, I saw only the last twenty minutes. Then there was the interval and the news, and then the other film.'

'What was that called?'

'It was *Meet Me in Rio*, with Joan Seymour and Broderick Davis.'

'When did that finish?'

'At five o'clock. I wanted to stay and to see the big film through, but it was already late, I was afraid that my father had already begun tea. So I bought an evening paper in order to pretend I had been out for one and went in through the front door.'

'This film, *Scarlet Witness*,' murmured Gently, 'is it the same one as I saw in London a fortnight ago? How does it end?'

Gretchen turned towards him, her hands snatching at each other. 'I did not see much of it . . . I do not remember. It was not very good.'

'But you saw the end of it?'

'It was . . . complicated.'

'Was it the one where they get taken off the island in a helicopter just as the volcano erupts?'

The two hands gripped till the knuckles whitened. 'No! It wasn't that one . . . I was worried about whether my father would find out, I did not see it properly.'

'They made an appeal after the one I saw – some fund for the maintenance of an aerial rescue force. Did they make an appeal here?'

'Yes – yes! There was an appeal for something. A man

spoke from the stage and they sent round boxes. I put something in.'

She bent her head away from him as though his eyes reacted upon her physically. Gently shrugged and felt in his pocket for a peppermint cream. She continued, without looking at him: 'The big film came on at a quarter to two and finished at a quarter past three. The other film started at half-past three and finished at five.'

Gently said: 'Thank you, Miss Huysmann, for such precise information.'

Hansom said: 'When you re-entered the house, whom did you see?'

'It was Susan. She was coming out of the passage from the kitchen.'

'What did she say to you?'

'She said, "Oh, I did not know that you had gone out," and then she told me that something was wrong with my father.'

'Did you go into the study?'

'No, after I was told I did not feel that I could. I sat down in the kitchen and Mrs Turner gave me some brandy to drink.'

'Then it wasn't you who hid the knife in the trunk?' demanded Gently suddenly. Gretchen writhed in her chair. 'I know nothing, nothing about that!' she exclaimed.

'And you wouldn't know if Fisher the chauffeur was in the house during the afternoon?'

A shiver ran through her dark-clad form, her eyes widened and her mouth opened. For a moment she stared at Gently horror-struck. And then it was over, as quickly as it had begun: the eyes narrowed, the mouth closed, the lips were forced deliberately into a tight line. 'I do not know, I was not here,' she said.

Gently sagged a little in his chair. He looked tired. 'How long has Fisher been chauffeur here?' he asked.

'Oh . . . three or four years.'

'Would you describe him as being honest and trustworthy?'

'Otherwise, my father would have got rid of him.'

'I am asking for your personal impression.'

'He is honest . . . I think.'

'What are your personal relations with Fisher, Miss Huysmann?'

'I do not see him, very much. Sometimes he is in the house to move things about. One day, he drove me to service at the cathedral, because I has a poisoned foot and could not walk there.'

'He is respectful and obedient?'

'Oh, yes.'

'Was he on good terms with your father?'

'I do not know – my father was not . . . a condescending man.'

'He had no reason to harbour a grudge against your father?'

'Oh, no.'

'The maid, Susan, is an attractive girl. Is there anything between her and Fisher?'

'. . . No! Nothing whatever!'

Gently's eyebrow rose the merest trifle and he transferred his gaze to the top of the far window. 'Would it be correct to say that you were in considerable fear of your father?'

'I do not know . . . fear.'

'You had observed how Peter was treated, how he was driven out and completely disowned. Did it not suggest to you that a similar fate might be yours on some other occasion?'

'Peter took money . . . he got married.'

'But you also disobeyed your father in the matter of going to the pictures.'

'That was very wrong of me, very wrong.'

'Miss Huysmann, were you deceiving your father in any other matters, perhaps more important ones?'

'I do not know how you mean!'

'You were very isolated here. You went out very rarely. You were denied all the usual facilities for meeting people and making friends. And you are twenty-seven. Did you propose to continue in this way of life indefinitely, or had you resolved to, shall we say . . . assert your rights, in some manner?'

'I cannot understand!'

'Your visits to the pictures, for instance, were they always made alone? Was it always to the pictures that you went?'

'Always – to the pictures! – always!'

'And always alone?'

'Every time I was by myself!'

'You were never accompanied by . . . Fisher, for example?'

A hot blush sprang into the pale cheeks. 'No! Never! Never!'

'Your association with him has always been that of mistress and servant?'

'How can you ask such things! How can you ask them!' Tears welled up in the dark eyes and she covered her face with her hands.

Gently said: 'I don't like asking these things, Miss Huysmann, any more than you like being asked them. But if justice is to be done, we must have a clear picture of all the events surrounding this crime. You may think that these questions are unnecessary, you may be tempted to answer them untruthfully; but remember that they are the steps by which a man may be brought to the gallows and that no personal feelings should be allowed to dictate what you will answer.'

She cried: 'It isn't true . . . I cannot help him!'

'You wish to answer that your association with Fisher is completely impersonal?'

She raised her face from her hands, agonized and tear-wet. 'Yes, that is my answer . . . O God! Please, let me go now, please!'

Hansom said: 'That stuff about the pictures – did it add up?'

Gently leant a freshly filled pipe to his lighter. 'No,' he said, 'it didn't. She didn't go to the pictures.' He gave a few puffs and adjusted matters with his thumb.

'Then you're reckoning that she was in the house during the afternoon?'

'It could be that.'

'And Fisher was there with her and she set him on to get rid of the old man and they swiped the money just for a blind. It's not a bad line at that!' exclaimed Hansom admiringly.

Gently smiled at the far-flung Pylades. 'You've got a lurid imagination,' he said.

'And young Peter comes in and nearly messes things up. They watch him quarrelling through the transom lights, and see the old man give him a note which might be traced and realize it's a pip. Fisher goes in and does the job, and then they slide out and collect alibis. Why, it's a natural!'

'And how about the knife in the trunk?'

'Oh blast, you can surely think of something to cover that!'

Gently's smile widened to include the still-vexed Bermoothes. 'It's an interesting conjecture. There's only one element lacking.'

'And what would that be?'

'Proof,' said Gently simply, 'there isn't a grain of it.' And he blew a playful little smoke-ring over his colleague's close-cropped head.

CHAPTER SIX

LEAMING BY DAYLIGHT was as handsome as ever. When he came in he immediately produced his gold cigarette case and offered everybody one of his hand-made cigarettes. Hansom and the constable accepted. Gently had only just puffed his pipe into flavoursome maturity. Leaming took a cigarette himself, tapped it on the case, twisted it between his lips and lit it with a slim, gold-plated lighter. Then he sat down, and with a jet of smoke from each nostril indicated that he was alert and attentive.

Gently said: 'You'll be able to tell me – who got the City's first goal yesterday? Was it Robson?'

Leaming glanced at him in surprise. 'It was Smethick, actually,' he said. 'He scored from a free kick after a foul on Jones S.'

Gently murmured: 'Ah yes, in the twenty-second minute.'

A correction seemed to hover on Leaming's lips, but eventually he said nothing.

'I don't suppose we shall need to keep you very long, Mr Leaming,' Hansom said. 'We'd just like to know a few routine details.'

'Glad to help you in any way.'

'What time did you leave the yard yesterday?'

Leaming thought and answered carefully: 'At twenty past one.'

'Were you the last person to leave?'

'Yes. I usually lock up personally.'

'Is the entire yard locked up, or only the office and buildings?'

'The office and buildings. But there is a boom across the entrance to prevent unauthorized vehicles entering and parking.'

'But that would not prevent persons from entering or leaving the yard?'

'It would not – there is an unlocked side-gate in any case.'

Gently asked: 'Isn't it tempting providence to allow free access to the yard in that manner?'

Leaming shrugged and breathed smoke. 'There's nothing to steal but timber. Nobody would manhandle a load of that right across the yard to the gate – especially under the eye of Mr Huysmann. His bedroom windows look down on the yard.'

Hansom continued: 'When did you last see Mr Huysmann?'

'He left the office at about ten past one. He looked into my office to say that he was going to London on Monday.'

'Did he say what for?'

'To pay Olsens' for the last quarter's shipments. Olsens' are our agents at Wapping.'

'Was it usual for Mr Huysmann to make payment in person?'

75

'Oh yes, invariably. And always by cash – it was one of his eccentricities.'

'About how much would the quarterly payment amount to?'

Leaming thought unhurriedly. 'This quarter's was eleven thousand three hundred and twenty-seven pounds plus some odd shillings, less three per cent for cash.'

'Did you notice anything unusual about Mr Huysmann yesterday morning?'

'Nothing in particular. He was a little – ah – agitated because his son was in town. I believe he thought that Peter only came to Norchester to annoy him, but that's by the way. He mentioned the will again and said that after Easter he proposed to call on his solicitors.'

'Did he lead you to suppose that he expected a visit from his son?'

'As a matter of fact, he did say something of the sort, or at least something which might be construed that way. He said (he had a peculiar way of speaking): "He'll find me ready for him, Leaming, *ja, ja*, he'll find me ready."'

'And you think it might have referred to an expected visit?'

'It might have referred to his intention to change his will, of course, but since then I've wondered.'

'Would you say that he stood in any fear of his son?'

'Oh, I don't know about that. He had acted, I think, a little unwisely towards Peter, and Peter had a temper, but to say he "stood in fear" is laying it on a bit.'

'But you would say that he was apprehensive?'

'He was always nervous when Peter was in Norchester.'

'To your knowledge, had Peter ever visited him before since he left home?'

'Not to my knowledge.'

'They had never met since Peter absconded with the money?'

'Never.'

Hansom stubbed the end of the hand-made cigarette into his ashtray and reached for his cigar case by way of afters. Leaming sat watching, handsome and unabashed, while the Inspector carved the tip off a Corona and lit it carefully all round. 'Hah!' said Hansom. Leaming smiled politely.

'Where did you go after you'd locked up?' continued Hansom.

'I went home for lunch.'

'Where's that?'

'I live at Monk's Thatch, at Haswick.'

'Do you live alone?'

'I have a housekeeper, a Mrs Lambert, and a gardener who comes in daily.'

'Were they there when you went home for lunch?'

'The housekeeper was, of course, but the gardener had knocked off. He came back later and I gave him a lift to Railway Road.'

'What time did you arrive home?'

'About a quarter to two.'

'What time did you leave again?'

'It was just on twenty to three – I was rather late. It isn't easy to get to the car park through the crowds.'

'And what time did you get to Railway Road?'

'It was just turned three. I dropped Rogers (that's my gardener) off at the station end and went on to park my car. By the time I'd done that it was quarter past and I missed the kick-off.'

Gently said: 'Are you a keen City supporter, Mr Leaming?'

Leaming gave a slight shrug. 'I suppose I am, really. I never miss a home match if I can help it and I sometimes manage the near away fixtures.'

'Then you will have a season ticket, of course?'

Leaming hung on a moment. 'Actually, no,' he replied. 'For me, half the excitement goes out of a match when I watch it from a seat in the stands. I love the hurly-burly and noise of the terraces. It sets the atmosphere of anticipation. To sit on a hard seat with my knees in someone's back and someone's knees in mine, to be detached from the drama taking place by a stooping roof of girders and galvanized sheet – no, I must have my terraces, or the game isn't worth the candle.'

'I like the terraces myself,' said Gently dryly. 'I wish I was as tall as you.'

Leaming laughed, pleased, and Hansom proceeded: 'At what time did the match finish?'

'At five to five. I got away at about a quarter past and went home to tea. Shortly after six you people rang me up and asked me to put in an appearance, which I did, straight away.'

Hansom said: 'I understand, Mr Leaming, that you feel strongly convinced of Peter Huysmann's innocence. Could you tell me what reasons you have for this?'

A tiny frown appeared on Leaming's handsome brow. 'Well, I suppose I haven't got what you'd call reasons. Not things like clues and evidence and that sort of thing. It's mostly a matter of personal feeling – I just know Peter so well that to ask me to believe he's done this seems ludicrous. I wish he were here now. I wish we could talk it over quietly with him. You'd soon see what I mean.'

'Have you any reason, then, for supposing that some other person was responsible?'

Leaming spread his hands, palms downwards, and placed them on his knees. 'It could have been almost anybody, really,' he said.

'How about Fisher – does he suggest himself as a suspect?'

'He would know that there was money in the safe.'

'How would he know that?'

'There's not much that servants don't know. He wouldn't know the amount was so large, of course. That was due to payments from the City Treasury on timber contracts to their housing estates. But he could easily have discovered that payment was made on the first of this month.'

'You do not think that Peter Huysmann belongs to the killer type. What would be your estimate of Fisher?'

'I don't know Fisher as well as I know Peter,' replied Leaming cautiously. 'It isn't fair to ask my opinion.'

'We should like to have it, all the same.'

'Well, there's a streak of brutality in the man. I wouldn't put it past him.'

'Can you tell us anything of his relations with the rest of the household?'

'I don't know that I can. He was an efficient chauffeur, knew his job, didn't get drunk, was always punctual. May have chased the women a bit – but there you are.'

'The maid Susan – did he chase her?'

'He may have done, though I doubt whether he had any success. Susan is well aware of her market value.'

'It is unlikely that Miss Huysmann had anything to do with him?'

Leaming laughed. 'You couldn't know how Miss Huysmann has been brought up. She reads nothing but her Bible. She wouldn't know what to do with a man if she had one.'

Gently said: 'How long have you been with the firm, Mr Leaming?'

'It will be ten years in the autumn.'

'Did you find Mr Huysmann a difficult man to work for?'

Leaming shrugged. 'You've probably been able to form an opinion of what he was like. When I first came, I thought I wouldn't last a month, but the salary made me stick it out.'

'It was a good salary?'

'Oh yes. One must give the old man his due. He's always paid the best wages in the trade – had to, I suppose, to get anybody to work for him. But that's not quite fair, though. He had really first-class business principles. He wanted a lot for his money, but he always paid generously for it, and right on the nail. Whatever he was like at home, you could trust him in business to the last farthing. That's how he built up a firm like this. Nobody was very fond of the man, but they all liked his way of doing business.'

'And would that sum up your attitude towards him?'

'I think it would.'

'You bore him no grudge for his treatment of you?'

'Good heavens, no! It was rather an honour to be manager of Huysmann's.'

Gently laid down his pipe and fumbled around for a peppermint cream. 'I believe you are a bachelor,' he said.

Leaming nodded.

'Would that be anything to do with Mr Huysmann?'

'Well, yes, I suppose it would. He preferred his staff to be unmarried.'

'Did that mean you would have lost your job if you had married?'

'Oh, I don't know about that, though he was quite capable of going to such lengths. But I never ran the risk.'

'It could be a very irksome situation, however.'

Leaming smiled complacently. 'There are ways of alleviating it.'

Gently bit a peppermint cream in halves. 'Such ways as Susan?' he enquired.

'One could go further and fare worse.'

'Which makes you positive that Fisher was having nothing to do with her?'

Leaming's smile broadened. 'I think you can discount Fisher in that respect,' he said. 'As I said before, Susan is well aware of her market value.'

'Ah,' said Gently, and ate the other half of the peppermint cream.

Hansom took a deep breath. 'Well,' he said, 'I don't think we shall require you any more for the present, Mr Leaming. Thank you for being so co-operative. We'll let you get away to lunch.'

Leaming rose to his feet. 'I'm only too glad to have been of any assistance. No doubt the Chief Inspector has told you that if you put Peter in the dock I shall be your number one adversary – but till then, call on me for any help I can give.' He smiled at both of them in turn and moved towards the door.

'Mr Leaming,' murmured Gently.

Leaming paused obediently.

'I should like to look over the firm's books.'

Leaming's brown eyes flickered, perhaps in surprise. 'I'll bring them over for you,' he said.

'This afternoon,' pursued Gently. 'I'll come back after lunch.'

'This afternoon,' repeated Leaming evenly. 'I'll have them here waiting for you.' He turned towards the door again.

'And Mr Leaming,' added Gently.

Leaming stiffened.

'I suppose you wouldn't know where one can buy peppermint creams in Norchester on a Sunday?'

Hansom pushed his chair back from the table and stretched his long, beefy legs. The constable shut his notebook and found another stringy cigarette. Gently got up and wandered towards the little pierced window.

Hansom said: 'Well, what do you know now?'

Gently shook his head slowly, still looking through the window.

'I guess this Leaming's the only lad with a pedigree alibi,' Hansom mused. 'Hit it where you like, it gives a musical note. What was that stuff about the books?'

'It's a wet day, I thought they'd be fun.'

'You didn't scare Leaming with it. I'll bet they check to five per cent of a farthing.' He dipped the long ash of his cigar into the ashtray. 'I haven't heard anything yet to make me think that young Huysmann isn't our man,' he said. 'You've started something with Fisher and the girl, but I don't think it's going to hold up the case. Mind you, I'll crack into Fisher. I'd like to know the ins and outs of that business myself. But I don't think it'll help you. I don't think he did it myself and I don't think you stand a dog's chance of proving it.'

Gently smiled into the window. 'There's so much we don't know,' he said, 'it's like a picture out of focus.'

'It focuses sharp enough for me and the super.'

'It's taking shape a little bit, but it's full of blind spots and blurred outlines.'

Hansom said challengingly: 'You're pinning your faith on Fisher, aren't you?'

Gently shrugged. 'I'm not pinning it on anybody. I'm trying to find out things. I'm trying to find out what happened here yesterday and what led up to it, and how these people fit into it, and why they answered what they did answer this morning.'

Hansom said: 'We're not so ambitious. We're just knocking up a case of murder so it keeps the daylight out.'

'So am I . . .' Gently said, 'only I like walls round mine as well as a roof.'

Still it rained. A black twig sticking out of the grille over the drain by the Huysmann house cut a rainbow wedge from the descending torrent. Gently stood a moment looking at it as he came out. Hansom had departed in the police car, carrying with him the constable and his notebook. He had offered Gently a lift and lunch at the headquarters canteen, but Gently preferred to remain in Queen Street.

'Looks like it's set in for the day, sir,' said the constable on the door. Gently nodded to him absently. He was looking now along the street towards Railway Bridge, sodden and empty, its higgledy-piggledy buildings rain-dark and forbidding. 'Where's Charlie's?' he asked.

'What's Charlie's, sir?'

'It's a snack-bar.'

'You mean that place down the road, sir?'

'Could be.'

'It's that cream-painted building about a hundred yards down on the other side.'

'Thanks.'

He plodded off towards Railway Bridge, his shoes paddling in the wet. They were good shoes, but he could feel a chill dampness slowly spreading underfoot. He shivered intuitively. The cream-painted building was a rather pleasant three-storey house of late Regency vintage. It had wide eaves and a wrought-iron veranda on the first floor, and had been redecorated probably as late as last autumn. It was only at ground level that the effect was spoiled. The sash windows had been replaced with plate glass and the door was a mixture of glass and chromium-plate. A sign over the windows said: CHARLIE'S SNAX. Another sign, a smaller one, advertised meals upstairs. Gently pressed in hopefully.

Inside was a snack-bar and several lino-topped tables, at which sat a sprinkling of customers. Gently approached the man behind the bar. He said: 'Are you serving lunch today?'

The man looked him over doubtfully. 'Might do you something hot, though we don't do meals on a Sunday as a rule.'

'Where do I go – upstairs?'

'Nope – that's closed.'

Gently took a seat at a vacant table by the door and the man behind the bar dived through a curtain behind him. It was not an impressive interior. The walls were painted half-cream and half-green, with a black line at high water mark. The floor was bare, swept, but not scrubbed. An odour of tired cooking-fat lingered in the atmosphere. The clientèle, at the moment, consisted of two transport drivers, a soldier, a bus-conductor and an old man reading a newspaper. The bar-tender came back.

He said: 'There's sausage and chips and beans and fried egg.'

Gently sniffed. 'I was hoping for roast pork and new potatoes, but never mind. Bring me what you've got.'

The bar-tender dived through the curtain again. Presently he came back with cutlery and a plate on which lay three scantly smeared triangles of thin bread, each slightly concave. 'Will you have a cup of tea to go on with?' he asked.

'Yes. No sugar.'

The tea arrived in a thick, clumsy cup. But it was fresh tea. Gently sipped it reflectively, letting his eye wander over the snack-bar and its inmates. This was where Fisher went for lunch. Fortified by a pint of beer, the chauffeur had come in to face his plate of sausage, chips, beans and fried eggs. What had he done while he waited? Read a newspaper? Talked? There was talk now between the two transport drivers.

'I got a late paper off the station . . . there's a bit in the stop-press about Scotland Yard being called in.'

'That's because the son hopped it, you mark my words.'

'D'you reckon he did it?'

'Well, you see what it said . . .'

'What did it say?'

'It said the police thought he could assist them in their

85

investigation. That's what they always say before they charge them with it.'

'They're a rum lot, them Huysmanns ... you don't know where you are with foreigners.'

The bar-tender sallied out with Gently's plate. Gently motioned to him to take the chair opposite. He hesitated suspiciously. 'You knew this young Huysmann?' enquired Gently blandly. The bar-tender sat down.

'Yep, I used to know him,' he said.

'What sort of bloke was he?'

'Oh, nothing out of the ordinary. You'd think he was English if you didn't know.'

'Used he to come in here?'

'He did before he went away, but he's been gone some time now. He had a quarrel with his old man before this lot happened.'

'Do you think he did it?'

'Well, I dunno. Might've done. He didn't look the sort, but you can never tell with these foreigners.'

Gently essayed a piece of sausage and chip. 'You know the chauffeur up there?' he asked through a mouthful.

'Who – Fisher?'

'That's his name, I believe.'

'Oh, he's often in here for something to eat. You know him?'

'I've run across him somewhere.'

'He's another rum card, if you ask me. He lives for women, that bloke. Thinks he's the gnat's hind-leg.'

'I heard he fancied the Huysmann girl.'

'He fancies every bloody girl. He was after our Elsie here till I choked him off.'

'Do you think there's anything in it?'

'I dunno. That girl Susan who works up there dropped something about it one night, but I don't pay any attention.'

Gently sliced an egg. 'Is she the blonde piece?'

'Ah, that's the one. She's a fancy bit of homework, I can tell you. But Fisher never got a look in there.'

'How was that?'

The bar-tender grinned knowingly. 'She's got a boyfriend out of his class. She runs around with Huysmann's manager, Leaming, his name is, a real smart feller. Fisher don't cut much ice while he's around.'

Gently doubled up a triangle of bread and butter and took a bite out of it. 'That get Fisher in the raw?' he mumbled.

'You bet it does – he'd give his arm to tumble her!'

'Mmn,' said Gently, masticating.

'I wouldn't mind a slice myself, if it comes to that.'

'Fisher been around lately?'

'He came in when he knocked off yesterday and had a meal.'

''Bout two, was that?'

'Nearer one, I should think. He hadn't got much to say for himself.'

The bar-tender was called back to serve a customer. Gently plodded onwards through the sausage. As he ate he fitted into place in his picture each new fact and dash of colour. Fisher, jealous of Leaming. Fisher, wanting to be Susan's lover. Susan, hinting at something between Fisher and Gretchen. 'He lives for women, that bloke . . . after our Elsie till I choked him off . . . Fisher never got a look in there . . . don't cut much ice while Leaming's around . . .' And Leaming had said, 'There's a streak of brutality in the man . . .'

The doorbell tinkled, and Gently looked up from his plate. It was Fisher himself who entered. Not noticing Gently, he swaggered over to the counter and ordered a cup of tea and some rolls, then stood there waiting while they were got for him. The bar-tender glanced at Gently, who winked back broadly.

Turning, Fisher saw Gently. He stopped stock-still. Gently nodded to him affably. 'Come and sit down,' he said, indicating the chair vacated by the bar-tender. 'I've thought up one or two more things I should like to ask you.'

CHAPTER SEVEN

A WHITE, EXPANSIVE April sun, low-tilted in its morning skies, looked down upon the rain-washed streets. In Chapel Field and the Castle Gardens birds were singing, thrushes, chaffinches, blackbirds, and on the steep southern and westerly slopes of the Castle Hill the daffodils looked down, proudly, consciously, like women dressed to go out.

Early traffic swirled up Princes Street and round Castle Paddock; the fast London train rumbled over the river bridge at Truss Hythe, swept out into the lush water-meadows of the Yar; passing over, as it did so, a stubborn little up-stream-making tug with a tow of five steel barges, on each of which was painted the name: Huysmann.

Onward puffed the little tug, bold as a fox-terrier, full of aggression and self-assurance, and onward crept the barges, phlegmatic, slow, till the cavalcade was in hailing distance of Railway Bridge. Then the little tug slowed down, trod water as it were, allowing the foremost barges to catch up with it. A man jumped out of the tug. He ran down the barges, jumping from one to another, till finally, coming to the last one, he loosed the sagging cable and cast her free. A shout ahead set the little tug puffing off on her interrupted journey, while the slipped barge, with the way left on her, was steered to a dilapidated-looking quay on the south bank.

Altogether, it was a smart and well-executed manoeuvre, thought Gently, watching it as he leaned over Railway Bridge. It was worth getting up early just to see it.

He crossed the bridge to watch the tug and its barges pass through the other side. A door in the rear of the tug's wheelhouse was open. Through it Gently observed a lanky figure wearing a peaked seaman's hat, a leather jacket and blue serge trousers tucked into Wellington boots. As he watched, the lanky man spun his wheel to the right. There was a tramp steamer on its way down.

Gently anticipated the warning hooter and got off the bridge. He stood by the railings to see the bridge rise, rolling ponderously, and moved further over to get a good view of the vessel as it surged by below. It was a bluff-bowed, clumsy, box-built ship, with a lofty fo'c'sle descending suddenly to deck level. The bridge and cabins aft were neat and newly painted, and the washing that hung on a line suggested that the captain had his family on board. The engines pounded submergedly as the steel cosmos slid through. There followed the bubbling and frothing under her stern. She was the *Zjytze* of Amsterdam.

Grumblingly the bridge rolled back into place and Gently, after a moment's pause, strolled over to the little glass box where the bridge-keeper sat. 'When did she come up?' he asked.

The bridge-keeper peered at him. 'Friday morning,' he said.

'What was she carrying?'

'Timber.'

'Where did she lie?'

The bridge-keeper nodded upstream to where the tug with its train of barges was edging in towards the quays. 'Up there at Huysmann's.'

'Is she a regular?'

'Off and on. She's been coming here since the war, and before that there used to be another one, but they say she was sunk in a raid. It's the same skipper, though.'

'Do you know his name?'

'It's a queer sort of name, something like Hooksy.'

'Thanks.'

Gently gave the departing vessel a last look and hurried away down Queen Street. A police car was outside the Huysmann house and Gently noticed, in a side-glance, that Leaming's car was parked inside the timber-yard. Constable Letts was on the door. 'Hansom inside?' asked Gently. 'Yes, sir. Been here for some time, sir.' Gently pushed in.

Hansom was in the hall, talking to a sergeant.

He said: 'Why, here he is, all bright and early.'

Gently said: 'There's a ship just left Huysmann's quays, the *Zjytze* of Amsterdam. Did you know about it?'

Hansom extended his large hands. 'A little bird told me about it last night.'

'And you've checked her?'

'That's sort of my job around here.'

'Well?'

Hansom took a medium-sized breath. 'They're football

fans,' he said, 'like everyone else round here, only more so.'

'How do you mean?'

'They went to London to see the Gunners.'

'All of them?'

'Yeah – one big happy family. The Skipper and Ma Hoochzjy, the son who's mate, the son who isn't mate, the son who's cook, three able-bodied cousins and a grandson who's cabin boy. They lit out for town at ten o'clock on Saturday, and got back on the 11.53 last night. They spent the night at the Sunningdale Hotel in Tavistock Place – I checked it – and went to Kew yesterday to give the tulips a once-over. They think our English tulips are *vonndervul*.'

'Did you check the vessel?'

Hansom gave a snort. 'Why do you think they've got customs at Starmouth?'

Gently shook his head in slow, mandarin nods. 'I don't *want* to have Peter Huysmann arrested, but as one policeman to another . . .'

'Good Lord!' gaped Hansom.

'. . . I think you'd better have the *Zjytze* checked before she clears Starmouth.'

Hansom was already doubling to the phone. 'I'll send some men out to Rusham!' he exclaimed. 'They'll have to wait there for the swing-bridge.' And he dialled viciously.

'Of course, he may be somewhere else entirely,' added Gently, 'he may even have grown a beard . . .'

They were sawing oak in the timber-yard. The smell of it, sweet with a sharpness and heaviness, carried into the street and even into the house, while the high-pitched whine of the saws, labouring at the hard, close grain, might be heard during intervals in the traffic as far as Railway Bridge. At the quays they were already busy with the barges. Two rattling derricks hoisted out bundles of rough-sawn planks and swung them to growing piles outside the machine sheds, where shouting men were stacking them. Close by an overhead conveyor trundled sawn-out stuff to a lorry. Pandemonium reigned in the great machine sheds. There were ranked the circular saws, buzzing at rest, shrieking with rage as they met the timber, whining viciously as they settled down to tear through it; the fiendish, screaming band-saws, temperamental and deadly; the soft, shuddering planers, cruel with suppressed power; and over all the sweet wholesome smell of sawn oak, of oak sawdust, of oak stacked in neat, separated piles.

Gently wended his way cautiously through this alien world. There was something shocking and amoral about so much terrible power, all naked; it touched unsuspected chords of destruction and self-destruction. He glanced curiously at the men who fed the lusting blades. They could not but be changed, he thought, they must partake of that feeling to some extent: become potential destroyers, or self-destroyers. He wished vaguely that such things were not, that timber could be produced by means other than these. But he could think of no other way, off-hand.

He came upon Leaming checking off a consignment of finished wood. Leaming grinned at him, a band-saw close by making oral communication impossible. Gently waited until he had finished checking, by which time also the band-saw had done ripping out scantlings.

'It's like this all day!' bawled Leaming.

'Doesn't it drive anybody mad?'

'They're mad when they come here – or else they wouldn't come!'

They walked on towards the comparative quiet of the planers, stopped to see the rough-sawn planks being driven over the steel bench with its wicked concealed knives. 'Tell me,' said Gently, 'do you get many suicides in here?'

Leaming threw back his head in laughter. 'No – they don't commit suicide here. They go away somewhere quieter for that.'

'Do you get accidents?'

'Not so many as you might think.'

Gently winced as a flying chip went past his face. He was aware of Leaming quizzing him, a little contemptuous. 'You soon learn to be careful when you're working a buzz-saw – mighty careful indeed. Most accidents happen when they're sawing up a tree with a bit of metal in it – an old spike that's grown into it or something. Sometimes the saw goes through it, but sometimes it doesn't.'

'What happens then?'

'The saw goes to pieces – and the pieces go a long way.'

Gently shuddered in spite of himself. Leaming laughed sardonically. 'Anything can happen here, any time. The miracle is that nothing much does happen . . .'

They walked out of the inferno and into the yard. Gently said: 'I suppose the old man Huysmann was rather like a buzz-saw in some ways.'

Leaming shot him a side-glance and then grinned. 'I suppose he was, though I never thought of him like that.'

'He buzzed and shrieked away happily enough until somebody put a spike in his log . . . and now nobody quite knows where the pieces will finish up.'

Leaming said: 'But there's one man with his neck right out to stop a lump.' His grin faded. 'I'd better get back to the office,' he said, and turned away abruptly. Gently stared after him, surprised at his sudden change of mood. Then he noticed somebody standing at the entrance to the office, a tall but rather furtive figure: someone who slipped inside as he realized that Gently's eye was on him. It was Fisher.

Two loaded transport trucks stood outside Charlie's, both from Leicester. Inside there was an air of briskness which had been lacking the day before. Most of the tables were occupied and in addition there was a group who stood around the fireplace (in which there was no fire) arguing. Their subject was the murder, which by now was getting front-page billing in all the popular dailies. One of the standing group held a paper in his hand. 'SLAIN MERCHANT – YARD CALLED IN', ran the headline. 'Son Still Missing . . .'

'You can say what you like,' said a transport driver, 'when they talk like that about someone, he's the one they want. They never do say anyone's the murderer till they've got their hands on him, but you can tell, all the same.'

'It don't mean that necessarily,' said a little stout man. 'I remember somebody who was wanted like that, but he got off all the same.'

'Well, this one won't get off . . . you listen to me. I'll have ten bob on it he hangs, once they get hold of him. You just read it again and see what they've got against him . . .'

There was a hush when Gently entered. Damnation, he thought, I must be growing more like a policeman every day. He ordered a cup of tea without sugar and added to it a cheese roll. The bar-tender's place had been taken by a girl in a flowered overall. She banged his tea down aggressively and retired to the far corner of the bar. Gently sipped tea and reflected on the hard lot of policemen.

Halfway through the tea the bar-tender put in an appearance. He nodded to Gently, and a moment later leant over the counter. 'Come upstairs, sir,' he said, 'there's something I think you'd like to hear about.'

Gently finished his tea and roll and went up the stairs. The bar-tender was waiting for him on the landing.

'Excuse me, sir, but you are Chief Inspector Gently of Scotland Yard, aren't you?' he asked.

Gently nodded, and sorted out a peppermint cream for digestive purposes.

'I thought you was him, when I remembered the way our friend Fisher acted when you spoke to him yesterday afternoon.'

'He was in his rights to tell me to go to hell,' said Gently tolerantly.

'Well yes, sir, I dare say . . .'

'What's your name?' asked Gently.

'I'm Alf Wheeler, sir.'

'Charlie to your pals?'

'Well, I do run this place, though there isn't no Charlie really – that's just what it's called. And I hope you don't think I was anyway disrespectful yesterday, sir, it's just I didn't know you were . . .'

'A policeman?'

'That's right, sir . . . though I ought to have guessed from the way you was leading me on.'

'Well, well!' said Gently, pleased, 'you're not going to hold it against me?'

'No, sir – not me.'

Gently sighed. 'It makes a change . . . what was it you wanted to tell me?'

The bar-tender became confidential. 'He was in here last night, sir.'

'Who?'

'Fisher, sir. He was a bit – you know – a bit juiced, and the girl Elsie and one or two of them was kidding him along, pretending they was scared of him – asking who he was going to do in next and that sort of thing. Quite harmless it was, sir – nothing intended at all.'

'Go on,' said Gently.

'Fisher, he begin to get all of a spuffle. "I could tell you a thing or two you don't know," he says, "and I could tell that b— Chief Inspector Gently something, for all his cleverness."

'"Why don't you tell us, then?" says the girl Elsie.

'"Never you mind," he says, "but you're going to see some changes round here shortly, you mark my words."

'"What sort of changes?" they say, but Fisher begin to think he's said enough. "You'll see," he says, "you'll see, and maybe it won't be so long either."

'"Hugh!" says the girl Elsie. "I 'spect he thinks he'll be manager at Huysmann's now."

'"Manager," he says, "I wouldn't be manager there for something. And another thing," he says, "there's people

97

cutting a dash today who may not be cutting one tomorrow,'' and after that he shut up and they couldn't get anything else out of him.'

Gently ate another peppermint cream thoughtfully. 'Would you say that the last remark referred to the manager?' he enquired.

'I thought it did, sir, and so did the others.'

'Have you any idea what he might have meant by ''changes''?'

'Well, you know what we was saying about there being something between him and Miss Huysmann? If that's the case, sir, then he's probably thinking, now that the old man is dead, that she'll take him on and make a man of him. I can't think what else he may have had in mind.'

'And then he would be in a position to deal summarily with Mr Leaming?'

'You bet he'll put a spoke in *his* wheel when he gets the chance.'

Gently shrugged. 'It depends a lot on Miss Huysmann's attitude,' he said. 'I wonder if, perhaps, he could be referring to something else . . .?'

He went down the stairs, followed by the bar-tender. A heated discussion amongst the group round the fireplace broke off as the door opened. Gently bowed to them gravely. 'Carry on, my friends . . . don't let us interrupt you,' he said. Twenty pairs of eyes from all parts of the snack-bar turned on him in silence. He shook his head sadly and went out.

The bright sun of the street struck in his eyes, making him blink. A steady stream of traffic was making in both directions, slowing at that point to get round the two parked trucks. A few yards further back Mariner's Lane disgorged a small, hooting van. Gently read the street sign with puckered eyes; at the same time he observed a figure standing in the gateway of the timber-yard. He turned directly and began walking casually towards the lane.

Mariner's Lane threaded the jungle between Queen Street at the bottom of the cliff and Burgh Street at the top. It was narrow and steep and angular. It began at the bottom by a derelict churchyard, carved its way past walls and slum property, with occasional vistas of desolate yards and areas, and threw itself at last breathlessly into the wide upper street, a bombed-site on one hand and a salvage yard on the other. It was a mean, seamy thoroughfare, part slum and part derelict: its only saving grace was the view it commanded – over the roofs of Queen Street, over the river, over the railway yards, as far as the bosky suburbs rising out of the easting Yar valley.

Gently plodded upwards with tantalizing slowness, pausing now and then to study his surroundings. He did not look back – at least, he did not appear to look back; but he looked long and hard at each miserable series of yards, and sometimes peered curiously at sparsely furnished windows. One of the many angular turnings brought him to Paragon Alley. It was a neglected little cul-de-sac about fifty yards long, with grass and ragwort growing out between the made-up surface and the pavement. One side was derelict, the other comprised of high walls and forgotten warehouses. Gently turned into it.

For a moment he did not see how anybody could live in Paragon Alley. It seemed too completely forgotten and neglected. And then he noticed, well down on the right-hand side, a warehouse over which were two curtained windows. It had access by a paintless side-door and two worn steps, and the number was chalked on the door: 5A.

Gently brooded before this footprint in the desert sands. 'It's quiet up the alley,' was what Fisher had said, 'there might have been someone about . . .' He turned to take in the blank face of the wall that closed the alley and the sightless windows that stared across the way. From the corner of his eye he saw the figure that slid out of sight at the entry . . .

There was a face at one of the windows, a dirty little urchin's face. It stared at Gently with mock ferocity.

'Hullo,' said Gently.

'Zzzzzzzz!' said the face, 'I'm Superman. I'm going to carry you away to the Radio Mountain.'

'Well, you'll have to come out here to do that,' said Gently.

'No, I won't – I'll get you with my magnetic ray!' A piece of stick came over the window-sill and levelled itself at Gently. 'Zzzzzzzzing!' said the face, 'zing! zing! Now I've got you!'

Gently smiled affably. 'What's your name?' he asked.

'I'm Jeff, the Son of Superman.'

'Do you often play in these old houses?'

'Mister, this is my headquarters. This is where I bring all my prisoners, after I've paralysed them with my magnetic ray.'

'Were you here on Saturday? Saturday afternoon?'

'Course I was. That was the day I caught Professor X and his Uranium Gang.'

Gently moved over, closer to the window. 'Do you

know who lives across there – over the warehouse?' he asked.

The little brow wrinkled itself ferociously. 'Course I know. He's my arch enemy. That's the hide-out of the Red Hawk, the biggest plane bandit in all England. That's where he builds his planes, mister, real ones, and then he goes out and shoots down other planes with gold in them. Oh, I've been watching him for a long time. One day I'm going to get him real good, and all the stolen gold he's got.'

'What was the Red Hawk doing on Saturday afternoon?'

'Saturday afternoon? That was when he shot down the mail-plane carrying all the gold. I tried to stop him, mister, I was firing the magnetic ray at him all the way down the alley. But do you know what I think?'

'What do you think?'

'I think he's got wise to the magnetic ray. I think he's got an atomic plate on him that stops it.'

Gently fumbled for his peppermint creams. 'Here,' he said, 'these are G-men hot-shots. They've got radio-active starch in them – they'll put sixty miles an hour on you.'

Superman took two and tried out one for effect. 'Gee – thanks, mister!' he exclaimed. 'I'll get that Red Hawk now, just you see.'

Gently said: 'Now this is important, Superman. What time did Red Hawk light out to rob the mail-plane on Saturday?'

Superman injected the second hot-shot. 'He went right away, mister, as soon as he'd come back for his Z-gun.'

'When was right away?'

'Right away after dinner.'

'And what time do you have dinner?'

'Oh, when my father gets back from the factory.'

'And after dinner you came right along here to headquarters?'

'You bet, mister. I'd got a special code message from Mars that Professor X was going to attack right after dinner. I wasn't going to miss him – he's been preying on s'ciety too long.'

· 'Did you see the Red Hawk come back again with the gold?'

Superman corrugated his brow. 'He's mighty cunning, is Red Hawk. He brought it in the back way – through all these old houses. But I saw him, mister. I saw him come in from my look-out post.'

'What time would that be?'

'Oh . . . I don't know. He'd been gone a good while, but it wasn't tea-time. I caught Professor X before tea-time.'

Gently pondered a moment. 'You can hear them at the football up here, I should think.'

'I'll say you can, Mister! You don't ever need ask how they're getting on, not up here.'

'They scored three times on Saturday. You hear them?'

'Course I did!'

'How many had they scored before the Red Hawk came back with the gold?'

'They'd just scored the second one as he was coming back.'

'You're sure of that, Superman?'

'Course I'm sure! I went up to my look-out post to see

if I could see it – you can see one of the goals, mister. And then I saw the Red Hawk creeping back through the houses.'

'What did he do?'

'Oh, he slipped into his lair with the gold and hid it with the rest, I 'spect. Then he went out again, down into the Lane, and asked somebody about the football.'

'And after that?'

'He just went off up the Lane.'

Gently administered another hot-shot. 'You're a good boy, Superman,' he said, 'you've got your head screwed on tight. What are you going to be when you grow up – a policeman?'

Superman's face wrinkled with disgust. 'Not me, mister. I'm really clever. I'm going to be the one who catches them when the police have given up . . . What's your name, mister?'

'Me?' Gently grinned. 'I'm Dick Barton Senior,' he said.

The Red Hawk stood at the entry to the alley, hands in pockets, scowling, disdaining any further concealment. The two-day growth of beard that darkened his face gave it a slightly sinister look. He still wore the beach-girl tie and American-style jacket, but had changed his slacks, which were formerly inconspicuous, for a pair of Cambridge-blue ones. He stood, as though barring Gently's egress. His eyes were aggressive and slightly mocking.

'You been asking questions about me?' he demanded.

Gently stopped, stared at him stolidly.

'Was that kid telling you a pack of lies?'

Gently remained silent.

'They aren't going to believe a kid. Nobody'll believe a kid – not that kid, anyhow. They had him in the home once. He's cracked.'

Gently said: 'Are you just going back to your flat?'

Fisher eyed him nastily. 'Suppose I am. There's nothing wrong with that, is there?'

Gently said: 'I'd like to come in and look it over.'

'Oh, would you? And s'pose I don't like policemen coming into my flat – what are you going to say to that?'

Gently shrugged. 'It's up to you,' he said. 'I could phone down for a search-warrant, if I thought it was worth it.'

Fisher swayed a little, his scowl deepening. 'All right,' he said, 'all right. You come in, Mr Chief Inspector Gently – you come in, and see where you get then.'

He led the way down the alley, Gently following a few paces in the rear. As they drew opposite the flat there was a warning cry from Superman. 'Watch out, mister! I've got the ray on him, but he's a desperate character!' Fisher made a threatening movement and Superman's face and ray-gun disappeared with great promptness. Fisher unlocked the door. There was a short section of dingy passage leading to a steep flight of steps. At the top of these was a dark landing from which opened three doors. Fisher threw them wide. 'There, Mr Chief Inspector Gently,' he said, 'go in and find some clues.'

Gently glanced around him impassively. The first room was a kitchen, combining, apparently, the duties of wash-room. The second was the bedroom, narrow, unornamented, its furniture an iron bedstead, a chair and a varnished chest-of-drawers. The third room was the living-room. It contained three chairs, a couch, a cupboard, a table and a stool. Its walls, from damp patches in which pieces of plaster had fallen, were decorated with coloured drawings of tight-skinned nudes taken from American magazines. Several nude photographs adorned the mantelpiece. The table stood under the window. On it stood several built-up scale models of aircraft, together with an untidy assemblage of balsa wood, tubes of cement, coloured tissue, piano wire and odd-shaped parts, amongst which lay a blunt-nosed skeleton fuselage. A printed sheet of balsa, partly cut out, was at the front of the table. Beside it lay an open cut-throat razor.

'Go on,' jeered Fisher, 'go right in and pull things about — I don't mind!'

Gently went in and slowly circumnavigated the room, touching nothing. Fisher watched him scowlingly from the doorway. 'You don't know anything,' he said, 'think you're so clever, coming from Scotland Yard, but you don't know a thing.'

Gently paused before the razor.

'That's it — have a good look at it! I go out cutting little girls' throats with that.'

Gently picked it up, tried the blade on his thumb and laid it down again. He turned and regarded Fisher distantly. 'What don't I know?' he asked.

'You don't know anything — that's what you don't know. You just think you do!'

'And what do I think I know?'

'You think you know I wasn't here when I said I was here, for a start.'

Gently said nothing.

'You think maybe I was at the house when it was done, don't you?'

Gently raised his eyebrows slightly.

'You think I heard them quarrelling and nipped into the other room and got a chair and watched it done – you think I could tell you how he got the knife off the wall and stabbed the old man as he was at the safe. That's what you think you know, Mr Chief Inspector Gently – that's what it is. But you don't know nothing really, nothing at all! And you're never going to know nothing, for all your cleverness.'

Gently took out a peppermint cream without moving his gaze from Fisher.

'You think you can find out things that Inspector Hansom can't find out. You've been bloody clever, haven't you? But there's as clever people about as you, don't you forget it. They know how much you can prove and how much you can't, and that's not a damn sight and never will be.'

Gently said: 'I might be able to prove that you're the father of Gretchen Huysmann's child.'

Fisher's mouth hung open. 'You'll *what?*' he gabbled.

Gently chewed his peppermint cream.

Fisher came closer. He thrust his face close to Gently's. There was anger and fear in his eyes. 'You're lying!' he spluttered, 'she isn't going to have a child!'

Gently chewed on.

'If she told you that, it's a lie – it's nothing to do with me!'

Gently swallowed.

'Anyhow, they can't prove things like that, not really. You're trying to trap me, that's what it is. You can't prove anything, so you're trying to make me say something by lying.'

Gently smiled at him seraphically.

Fisher breathed hard. 'You don't know anything!' he repeated fiercely, 'you only think you know!'

Gently placed a hand firmly on Fisher's chest and pushed him to one side. 'Think about it,' he said, 'take an hour off and think about it.'

He went down the stairs. From the top Fisher shouted after him: 'You can think what you like . . . you can't prove it!'

Gently completed his climb to Burgh Street and stood for some minutes by the bombed-site, partly to see the view and partly to get his breath back. A steep climb like that came as a warning that retirement was not so very far ahead. And then, he thought, I'll buy a cottage some-where, quite away from all superintendents with bad cases of murder, and fish . . . Having got his breath, he set off down the hill again. Near the bottom, as he was passing the ruined shell of an old factory-building, he heard a slight movement high above his head. He jumped without stopping to look. At the same moment a fragment of masonry about the size of a football crashed on to the pavement where he had been walking, bounced once and trundled away down the steep slope.

Gently stood motionless, pressed against the wall. There was a sudden clambering and rush of footsteps on the other side. Up the hill, down the hill the wall stretched blindly, completely without access. The foot-steps died away in the distance.

Gently picked up the fragment of masonry and placed it carefully at the side of the pavement. It weighed nearly half a hundred-weight. 'You can think what you like,' he quoted to himself, 'but you don't know nothing . . . and you can't prove it.' He fed himself a peppermint cream and walked on down the Lane.

CHAPTER EIGHT

T HE LATER LUNCH-TIME fly-sheets carried the news: PETER HUYSMANN CAUGHT. It was scanned by typists in snack-bars and discussed by housewives over their lunch-time coffee. The heavy, red-faced man who sold papers outside the bank shouted: 'Huysmann Taken Off Ship – Latest!' – and sold the thick sheaf under his arm as quickly as he could take the money. Two painters on a cradle high above the Walk heard his cry. 'Ted, get you down after a paper,' said the elder one, 'I used to know young Huysmann when he was knee-high to a tin of paint.' Ted went down the scaffolding like a monkey, but by the time he got to the pavement the papers were all sold. So he had to go round to the door of the printing shop and wait while the grumbling machines flapped out a fresh, warm-smelling edition.

'CAUGHT WHILE FLEEING COUNTRY' ran the revised headline, 'PETER HUYSMANN ON DUTCH SHIP BOUND FOR AMSTERDAM: Intercepted by Police at Haswick.' It continued: 'Peter Johann Huysmann, 28, son of the murdered Norchester timber-merchant, was discovered this morning hiding in the Dutch motor-vessel *Zjytze*, which was returning to its home port of Amsterdam after discharging a cargo of timber at Norchester. Wanted by the police for questioning in connection with the death of his father, Huysmann was discovered concealed in a hold when the vessel was intercepted and searched by the Yar River Police patrol boat at Haswick. Captain Hoochzjy, master of the *Zjytze*, in a statement to the Norchester City Police, denied all knowledge of the presence of Huysmann on board his vessel. Huysmann was taken to Norchester City Police Station. He was given a meal of bacon and fried sausages in the Police canteen . . .' And there was a photograph of Peter in his riding helmet, a bad one, deliberately chosen for its villainousness.

The elder painter scrutinized the photograph broodingly. He removed the tab-end of a Woodbine. 'Always something queer about that fellow,' he said, 'never quite like you and me, he was . . .'

Gently found Hansom closeted with the super in the latter's neat, bare office. 'He's got that look about him,' Hansom was saying, 'you know, it gets to be an instinct.'

The super rose as Gently came in. 'I'm glad you're here,' he said. 'Judging from the reports I've had in, you've put a finger on some complications which will need a thorough going over. At first – and I don't mind admitting it – I thought you were just being awkward. But I see now there are points here that would be a gift to the defence unless we get them straightened out first. Also, I think they will help us. If we can get the chauffeur to talk, our case is fool-proof.'

Hansom leered at Gently, but said nothing.

Gently said: 'You won't have charged him yet?'

'I'm going to charge him now, when we have him in.'

Gently said: 'May I offer some advice?'

The super glanced at him sharply, frowning. 'I'm always willing to take advice – sound advice.'

Gently's face was completely expressionless. 'My advice is not to charge him with murder,' he said.

Hansom let out a bellow. The super exclaimed: 'But good lord, Gently, it's impossible – completely impossible!'

Gently proceeded smoothly: 'I know it's a great deal to ask, and I wouldn't suggest it except for the best possible professional reasons. But, for your own sake, I advise you not to charge him.'

'I'm sorry, Gently, but it's completely out of the question.'

'You mean we should just question him and let him go?' yapped Hansom, 'just like that – with a conviction staring him in the face?'

Gently pursed his lips. 'I was not suggesting that,' he said.

'Then what are you suggesting?' snapped the super. 'To let him go now is as much as my post is worth and if I don't charge him, I can't hold him. What possible alternative have I?'

'You can hold him on a charge of unlawful possession.'

'Unlawful possession?'

'You found a bank-note in his caravan which was one of those stolen from the safe. I don't think you'll get a conviction, but it's enough to hold him on. And, it's one thing to fall down on a case of unlawful possession, quite another to fall down on a case of murder.'

'You know something that's not in these reports?' demanded the super, like the crack of a whip.

Gently sighed. 'I do,' he said.

'And what is that?'

'It's a lot of little things that I couldn't prove to your satisfaction, but they keep adding together in a way that doesn't point towards Peter Huysmann.'

'Then where do they point?'

'I don't want to be positive about that, yet.'

'You don't know?'

Gently shrugged his shoulders. 'I think it's safest to say that.'

'But, good heavens, Gently, what am I to think? You realize that there's people above me who want to know chapter and verse the reasons for my decisions? What am I going to tell them?'

'You could tell them you wanted a little more time.'

'But these reports speak for themselves.'

Gently felt around in his pocket hopefully and produced a part-worn peppermint cream. 'It's a very good case against Huysmann,' he said; 'if you could put him in dock tomorrow, you would get a conviction. Unfortunately you can't do that, and by the time you can, to the best of my judgment, there won't even be a case of unlawful possession against him. That's why I'm offering this advice, which you needn't accept.'

The super stabbed a glance at Hansom and exploded: 'Blast you, Gently! Can't you understand my position? My men have done a good job and they look to me to back them.'

Gently continued: 'If you do accept my advice it may be a help in clearing this matter up.'

'It is cleared up!' snarled Hansom.

'It will suggest to the culprit that we aren't satisfied. We may get a lead out of it.'

The super turned his back on them and fumed at the closed window. 'I wish to God I'd been a whelk-seller! I wish to God I'd stopped in the bloody Army! Would anybody in his right mind be a police superintendent?' He swung round on Gently. 'Let's get this straight – you want me to stand up my men and fob off the powers that be because you've got some blasted intuition – that's it, isn't it?'

'Not intuition,' murmured Gently, 'just judgment based on experience.'

'Intuition!' barked the super. 'Listen, Gently. Can you give me one good solid reason why Huysmann is not the murderer?'

'I think so, if you really want one.'

'*Want* one! Who am I supposed to be – the charwoman?'

Gently rubbed his chin with a stubby finger. 'An hour or two ago some interested person tried to drop some masonry on my head,' he said reluctantly. 'It was a large lump, and it wouldn't have bounced. Now why should anybody want to do that to a policeman?'

'I could tell you!' Hansom yipped.

'You mean they tried to kill you?' demanded the super.

'I'm afraid they did. Which seems to indicate that somebody has grown dissatisfied with the course of my investigations – that somebody is deeply interested in having Peter Huysmann convicted. There can't,' added Gently, 'be more than one reason for that . . . can there?'

★ ★ ★

Peter Huysmann had been fed and washed, but there had been no time to shave him. A mist of blond beard surrounded his rather long, drawn face and a darkness and sunkenness of the eyes betrayed the fact that he had slept very little in the past forty-eight hours. He was still wearing his overalls, now soiled and stained with oil: their being open at the neck gave him an unexpectedly boyish appearance. He was brought in by two constables. Parsons, the shorthand constable, had already taken his place.

'Sit down, Huysmann,' said the super, not unkindly, indicating a chair placed in front of his desk. Peter sat down with some awkwardness, placing his hands on his knees. He shot defensive glances at Hansom and Gently, who flanked the super right and left. His mouth was set in a drooped, quivering line.

The super cleared his throat. 'First of all, I am charging you, Peter Huysmann, with being in unlawful possession of property, namely a bank-note, removed from a safe, the property of your father, the late Nicholas Huysmann.'

Peter stared at him in momentary surprise, but probably supposing this to be some sort of prelude to a graver charge, said nothing. The super continued: 'Do you wish to say anything in answer to this charge? You are not obliged to say anything, but whatever you say will be taken down in writing and may be used in evidence.'

'Though not necessarily against you,' added Gently, in the pause that followed.

Peter looked from one to the other of them, still not quite able to follow the turn things were taking.

'Do you wish to say anything?' repeated the super.

Peter licked his lips. 'Yes,' he said, 'I – I'd like to tell you everything – all I can tell you.'

His voice was slightly harsh, but contained almost no accent. 'You'd like to make a statement?' asked the super.

'Yes, I'll make a statement. But I didn't take the bank-note – it was given to me.'

'You plead not guilty to the charge?'

'My father gave it to me just before I left.'

The super picked up a pencil and began doodling on a pad in front of him. 'Before you make your statement I would like to caution you once more. You are quite within your rights to say nothing and we have no power to demand that you shall. You do so at your own risk. I'm not saying this to stop you making a statement, but simply to warn you that you needn't if you feel it may incriminate you in a possibly graver charge. I can't put it plainer than that. It's up to you.'

Peter said: 'Thank you . . . but I want to tell you everything that happened.'

He licked his lips again and looked across at the constable with the notebook. Gently wondered: did they tell his wife or did she see it first in the lunch-time papers?

'You've found out how I left home,' said Peter, 'you know that my father and I weren't on good terms. It was my marriage he couldn't forgive – I was to have married the daughter of a merchant in Rotterdam, somebody rich. They'd worked it all out when I was in the cradle. When I married Cathy I just about ceased to be a son of his.

'It was pretty hard for me, never having had to get my living before. I knew how to drive a truck, so I got a job with a small transport firm at King's Lynn, and that went on for about three months. But the driver I was with got mixed up in a robbery – I lost my job and nearly went to

114

prison as an accessory. After that I got in with the fair people and learned to do an act. It didn't pay very well, so I persuaded Clark – he's my boss – to let me practise the Wall, and I got so good at it that he took me on as his number one rider.'

Hansom said: 'What was the act you learned that didn't pay very well?'

Peter hesitated. 'It was just one of the little side-show acts.'

'Anything like knife-throwing?'

'It *was* . . . knife-throwing.'

'Ah,' said Hansom, 'little details like that help to fill in the picture, you know. Don't leave them out.'

Peter flushed, his lip quivering. He went on, a little sullenly: 'I'd written to my father once or twice since I went away, but he never answered. My only contact was with Gretchen, whom I saw sometimes when I was in Norchester with the fair. And I used to write to her, addressing the letters to the maid Susan. Then two weeks ago, when the fair was at Lincoln, Clark offered me a partnership in the Wall if I could find up five hundred pounds. It was a very liberal offer . . . the Wall would clear a hundred pounds in a good week. I told him I would see my father when we got to Norchester.'

The super said: 'What made you think your father would let you have the money?'

Peter shrugged. 'I don't know. We were just coming to Norchester again, so I thought I would give it a try. Five hundred pounds was not much to my father . . . I thought he would lend it to me. First I sent a note to my sister, arranging to see her as soon as we got into town. She wasn't very hopeful. My father was still talking of changing his will and he had been in an irritable mood of late – perhaps because he knew I was coming to town.'

Gently said: 'Could there have been any other reason why he was irritable?'

'There was business, of course . . .'

'Do you know of any particular business reason which might have caused it?'

'He used to imagine there was a leakage somewhere. But that had been going on for years . . . I think it was a delusion. My father was a very suspicious man.'

'Did he suspect anyone in particular?'

'I don't think so.'

'Do you know how the wages he paid compared with those paid by the trade in general?'

'I couldn't say exactly, but he was not the sort of man to pay more than the minimum rate.'

'Would he have paid more than that, say, to his manager?'

'No, he couldn't have done: I can remember Mr Leaming complaining that he was getting only two-thirds of what some managers were paid.'

'You are positive of that?'

'Quite positive.'

'Did it never seem strange to you that Mr Leaming should not transfer to a firm where he would be better paid?'

'He had a reason for that. Before he came to us he was with a firm called Scotchers' which went bankrupt. There was no blame attached to Mr Leaming, but he found it difficult to get a position afterwards . . . he was the first manager to last with us for more than twelve months.'

116

Gently nodded his mandarin nod to signify that he had done. Peter licked his lips again and continued.

'After I'd spoken with Gretchen I thought I'd try to raise the money somewhere else. There was a firm called Trustus advertising in the local paper, so I went to them and told them the position. At first I thought I was going to get it. When they understood that I was the son of Nicholas Huysmann they were very favourable. But once they realized that I was on my own and without a fixed address it was different . . . even though I brought the last balance sheet to show them. I went to another firm after that, Goldstein in Sheep Lane, but it was the same there. So I decided to go through with my original plan.

'My father was usually busy in the yard on Saturday mornings, so I waited till the afternoon, which he was in the habit of spending in the study going over his books and the like. Clark scrubbed one of the performances at the Wall so that I could have an hour off. I didn't tell Cathy where I was going because I knew she would be upset . . . it would be time enough to tell her if I got the money. I left the fairground at about quarter past three.'

'What makes you sure of the time?' interrupted the super.

'There was a performance at three – they last about ten minutes. By the time I'd got out of my overalls and straightened up it would be about quarter past. I went straight down Queen Street and knocked on my father's door.'

Gently said: 'Did you notice if there were any vehicles parked in the vicinity?'

'I can't remember any. There was still quite a bit of traffic going down to the football match.'

'Did you see anybody you recognized, or any vehicles you recognized?'

'I wasn't thinking much about other people . . . Susan answered the door, and I told her why I had come. I also asked her where Gretchen was. She told me that my father was in the study and that Gretchen was upstairs in her room. I went along to the study, knocked and entered.

'My father was sitting at the table facing the door. He rose as I entered.'

'What did he say?' demanded Hansom.

'He said something like: "You! I was expecting you to turn up one of these fine days!" I replied that I had not come to annoy him but about a business matter.'

'What did he say to that?'

'He said that I hadn't any business to come about and that I could take myself off again. I did my best to smooth him down so that he would listen to me. I admitted that I had been very much in the wrong, and that I did not expect his forgiveness, and let him give me a thorough dressing-down without saying a word. After he had cooled off a little bit I mentioned that I was in the way of setting up in business on my own.'

'How did he take that?'

'He took it a good deal better than I expected. I went into details about the partnership, showed him the balance sheet and eventually touched on the five hundred pounds. He said, "Yes, I could see that coming," and got out the safe key. I could hardly believe in my good luck. He went over and opened the safe and took out a packet of five-pound notes. Then he came back and put them on the table between us. "There," he said, "there's five hundred pounds, my little man. Let us say that is what you were worth to me two years ago. But you've depreciated," he said, "you've gone down in the market, my son. Today, you are worth only one per cent of your value two years ago. You have taken money, ha, ha! You have run away, ha, ha! And ... you have married!" Upon which he stripped off the top note and thrust it into my hand. "That is your value to me, my son," he said, "you have it now, and that is all you will ever have."

'For a moment I just stared at him, unable to credit it. The next, all my self-control had gone. Everything that had been stored up for two years came out in a rush ... everything. I told him just what I thought of him. I couldn't help it. I have a very bad temper ... we both had ...'

'Can you remember anything of what you said?' asked Gently.

'I said that he was unnatural – that he had sold his soul – that he had no more human feelings left: and I called him names ... hypocrite ... miser ... satyr ...'

'Did you refer to the bank-note?'

'Yes. I told him there'd be a time when that note came back to roost ... with interest.'

'What did you mean by that?'

'I'm not quite sure. I had some idea of returning it in such a way that he would regret it ... I don't know how.'

The super said: 'Think carefully, now. Was there any violence on either side during this quarrel?'

'No, none.'

'Was any offered?'

'No ... my father raised his hand once, but that was all.'

119

'Very well. Go on with your statement.'

'In the end I flung out of the side door and left him to it. The last thing he said was that if I ever showed my face there again he'd have me put in charge.'

'Why did you leave by the side door?' asked Hansom.

'It happened to be open, and I wanted to get out quickly. I went back to the fairground in a flaming temper. I told Cathy what had happened, which upset her, I'm afraid: it wasn't fair, but I had to let off steam somehow. Anyway, I cooled down a bit and had a cup of tea, and then went over to the Wall for my next ride.'

'What time was that?' Gently enquired.

'It was timed for four-thirty.'

'Where did you put on your overalls – at the Wall?'

'No . . . I put on this spare pair. I had them at the caravan. I tore the seam of the other pair when I took them off.'

'Did you see anybody you knew as you crossed the fairground?'

'I shouldn't have noticed them if I did. I saw Clark, who told me not to take it to heart too much – he said he'd got a pal in London who might put up the money for me. And then I got on with my rides. I rode at four-thirty, five, five-thirty and six. After the show at five I went back to the caravan and had something to eat . . . also, I tried to cheer Cathy up. By the six ride I'd pretty well got over it. And then I went out and bought a paper . . .

'I saw it directly because I looked at the stop-press for the football results. It struck me absolutely numb, like a blow on the head . . . it almost seemed that I must have done it myself. I felt as though I were . . . doomed.'

'Did it not occur to you that the best thing to do would be to come straight to the police?' asked the super sternly.

'But what would they think? What could they think? Everything was so much against me that I could hardly believe myself . . . The quarrel, that must have been heard by everyone in the house – perhaps other people; my relations with my father – my need of money – his intention of changing his will – it was all well known. And then, for it to have happened directly after the quarrel . . . it seemed that I was caught up in some terrible mechanism. There was only one thing left to do, and I did it.

'That evening I hid amongst some derelict buildings near Burgh Street. As soon as it was dark I made my way out of town towards Starmouth. I didn't know quite what I should do, but I felt I should be safer out in the country. I spent the night in a cart-shed somewhere and tried to think things over and make a plan. There was just a chance that the police would find the murderer quite quickly, that I might not have been suspected at all. In that case I intended to give myself up. But if they did not, then it was as good as committing suicide and I resolved that somehow I must get out of the country. At first I thought I would go on to Starmouth, but it was a long way. Then I thought of the timber-boats that came up to Norchester. Some of them were Dutch, and as you know, I am Dutch by extraction and speak the language perfectly. If I could get on one of those to Holland I should be safe, and later on I could get a message back to Cathy and have her brought over to me.

'I hid all Sunday in some woods not far from the city.

In the morning I had ventured out to some cottages and stole a newspaper from a letter-box. I was convinced from what I read in it that I must get away. When the night came again I worked my way back into the city, keeping to all the back roads and side lanes, and made a reconnaissance along Riverside. There I found the *Zjytze*. I knew her well – also, she was empty, which meant that she would soon be on her way home. So I crept round into the timber-yard and got aboard her.'

The super slashed parallel lines across a pattern he was building up on his pad. 'You realize, of course, the immediate construction we were obliged to place on your actions?' he asked.

Peter's hand opened appealingly. 'I know . . . I know . . . but what else could I have done? It was not my life that was wanted . . . yet who would believe that?'

'We were bound to catch you in the long run. It would have been best to come to us straight away.'

'I don't know . . . one must try to save one's life.'

Hansom said: 'Was it true that Hoochzjy didn't know you were on the vessel?'

'I could not risk letting him know, not until we were clear of England. I know him well and I don't think he would have given me up; but I was not going to risk it.'

Gently said: 'I'd like to go back a little bit. You said just now that "the quarrel must have been heard by everyone in the house". Whom did you have in mind?'

'There was Susan and my sister . . . perhaps others.'

'Did you see your sister?'

'No, but Susan told me that she was there.'

'Who were the others?'

'Other servants, perhaps . . .'

'Did you see anyone else at all besides Susan and your father?'

'No.'

'Or hear anything, or see any signs of anyone else?'

'Not . . . really.'

'What do you mean by that?'

'I can't tell you anything definite, but while I was talking to Susan in the hall I had the impression that there was somebody upstairs on the landing.'

'You saw them?'

'It is very dark in the hall. I can't be certain.'

'Did you actually look in that direction?'

'Yes, but I didn't see anything. It may be I thought I heard a movement up there, or perhaps I actually did catch sight of somebody out of the corner of my eye; anyway, they had gone when I looked.'

'And you proceeded with the impression that there was another person in the house besides yourself, your father and Susan?'

'If I thought about it at all, I thought it was Gretchen.'

'But you did proceed with that impression?'

'Yes, I did.'

'Coming now to your interview with your father. Whereabouts did you stand during that interview?'

'Oh, by the table most of the time.'

'You are speaking of the large table that stands roughly in the centre of the room, not far from the safe?'

'Yes.'

'You were on the near side and your father on the far side?'

'Yes.'

'Then you had your back to the inside door?'

'Most of the time.'

'During that interview, did you hear anything that might lead you to believe there was somebody outside that door?'

'I can't think of anything.'

'Would you have noticed, for instance, if your father looked at it in a particular way, suggesting that he had heard or seen something?'

'I wouldn't have noticed.'

Gently paused for a moment. 'From where you were standing, you could see through the outer door into the garden, also the outer gate, also part of the summer-house through the small window?'

'I suppose I could, but I didn't notice them much.'

'Can you say whether the outer gate was open or closed?'

'It seemed to be closed, but when I went out I found it was slightly ajar.'

'You saw nobody in the garden at any time?'

'No.'

'Nor in the summer-house?'

'No.'

'You would not have noticed if the summer-house door was opened or closed?'

'Yes, I did. It was standing half-open.'

'Was there anybody in the timber-yard when you went through it?'

'Nobody.'

'Or any vehicle?'

'None.'

Gently spread out his stubby fingers and placed the tips

together in strict sequence. 'Your sister,' he said, 'she does not appear to have many acquaintances.'

Peter shrugged and shook his head. 'It is my father's fault . . . she does not know anybody except a few people she meets at church.'

'What sort of people are they?'

'Oh . . . elderly, not very interesting.'

'Has your sister any admirers to your knowledge?'

Peter's long face twisted in a wry smile. 'There was a young fellow once. He was called Deacon . . . he worked in a solicitor's office. But my father soon put a stop to that. It happened several years back.'

'Your father had a plan for marrying you to a Dutch girl. Had he any such plan for Gretchen?'

'No! That would have cost money . . . in Holland she would have required a dot. With me, of course, it was different.'

'If she had a lover, would you expect to be in her confidence?'

'Well . . . that's hard to say. Gretchen is very strange and very religious. She tells me most things, but not all. If it were anything serious I think she would tell me.'

'Have you ever had any suspicions, say of members of the household . . . or the staff?'

'None at all. But I have been away two years.'

'Would you be surprised to hear that Gretchen had, in fact, a lover?'

Peter stared hard at Gently. 'No,' he said, 'I don't think so. Her religion . . . it is the sort that would easily turn to something else . . . a substitution for it.'

'Would you say it was true that she was very much afraid of her father?'

'Everybody was afraid of my father.'

'But Gretchen, perhaps, especially?'

'In her position, I suppose she was . . .'

The shorthand constable closed his notebook and Gently, unable to smoke in the super's office and out of peppermint creams to boot, stretched himself and sighed largely.

'He's clever,' said Hansom, 'he's dead clever. And he can tell a story.'

The super tore off his sheet of doodlings. 'It's the sort of statement an innocent man might make if he were honest . . . and a guilty man if he were clever. It doesn't seem to have helped you much, Gently.'

'I wouldn't say that.' Gently permitted himself the ghost of a smile. 'At least we've got an indication that there was some other person in the house, besides those we know of.'

'But that's all you've got, and you've been hammering away at it all through the questioning. The really important point, that somebody was at hand during the quarrel, you've drawn a blank on.'

'There's the chair-marks and the finger-prints,' mused Gently.

The super made impatient noises. 'You know how much that's going to impress a jury. As part of a chain of evidence it would stand up, but taken on its own it would only furnish an opportunity for sonic forensic fireworks by the counsel. Look here, Gently' – the superintendent adopted a friendly tone – 'let's have young Huysmann back and charge him properly, and forget all this other business. I know you think he's innocent, but he's got himself into a mess and it's up to his counsel to get him out of it, not us. We're just here to get the facts and we've got them . . .'

Slowly Gently shook his head. 'We haven't got them . . . not all of them. For one thing there's the money, and for another there's the gentleman who tried to bounce masonry on my head . . .'

The super's jaw moved out a good half-inch. 'Very well, Gently, have it your way,' he snapped, 'but by God, you'd better be right! I'm giving you forty-eight hours before I charge young Huysmann: after that, you're on your own.'

Gently met the super's eye with a look of mild reproof. 'I do wish you people would realize that I'm on your side,' he said.

CHAPTER NINE

EVEN HIS OWN Chief seemed just a little bit against him, thought Gently, dropping the receiver on a long telephone consultation. Chiefy had seen the papers and left instructions for Gently to ring him. 'I know I can trust you, Gently,' he had said, 'and you can't tell me anything about the attitude of provincial superintendents. But for heaven's sake bear in mind that you're unofficial and don't stir up trouble. If the local gendarmerie think they've got a case, well, just let them keep right on thinking – if they haven't, they'll find out soon enough when it gets to court.'

Which is as good as telling me to drop it, thought Gently . . .

He looked down at the dusky city with its ten thousand lights, with the moving jewels that were cars and the sauntering shop-windows that were buses. In the market place they were busy packing up, flowers and vegetables were being dispatched on hand-carts to the subterranean vaults under the Corn Hall. Down London Street came a news-boy with the Late Night Finals: No Murder Charge in Huysmann Case, Final! Final! The day was over, the business was done. Now it was time to pack up, to have tea, to slacken the tireding wheels of commerce. And then there was the pictures or the Hippodrome . . .

Gently walked down by the Guildhall and crossed over to the brightly lit foyer of a small café, the Princess. It had a bowl of fruit in one window and a dish of cakes in the other, and both seemed, to a hungry Gently, well up to chief inspectorial standards. He went in. It was a pleasant, intimate place with oak beams and nooks and a large fireplace in which slumbered a mature fire and a wireless turned down low spoke of football in the midlands. He selected a small, nooky table within fire-range and glanced down the menu.

A tall pretty waitress came to him.

'Mixed grill,' said Gently, 'with two helpings of fried onion. What are the sweets like?'

'The fruit salad is very good, sir, and there's clotted cream today.'

'Cow cream?' asked Gently cautiously.

'Oh yes, sir.'

'Ah!' said Gently, 'well, have it all ready. And I'll finish up with biscuits and Stilton and white coffee. And by the way, I like a *lot* of Stilton . . .'

The wireless programme had changed to music, South American, with subtle, nostalgic rhythms. Gently expanded himself towards the benevolence of the fire. Forty-eight hours and then he was on his own . . . with full police non-co-operation. Of course, the break might come sooner. The fact that Peter hadn't been charged right away might set things moving. It would certainly worry somebody. But if it didn't, what then? It didn't need the super to point out that Gently was butting his head against a wall. The wall was only too obvious. It loomed up everywhere. Try as he might, he always came across it at last, solid and indestructible, surrounding the blank on the map with unswerving determination. But the very fact that it was there, that it kept occurring, was significant: if Gently couldn't get beyond it, at least he had become familiar with its direction and extent.

And the key-stone in the wall was Fisher. It was Fisher who had to crack. Take away Fisher, and the whole obstinate construction would collapse and reveal its secrets, whatever they were. All Gently's mature instincts told him that – break Fisher, and the rest would fall into place. But if Fisher kept his nerve and did nothing foolish . . .

The waitress came back smiling with an interesting-looking tray. Gently called for rolls and went stolidly to work on his mixed grill. He ate seriously and with enjoyment. Food was one of those dependable pleasures, like smoking.

He thought of Gretchen. Had he been right with that shot in the dark, about her being pregnant? It had shaken Fisher, at all events, and confirmed Gently's belief that he was her lover. But why should he have expressed fear? If it was his plan now to marry Gretchen and succeed to the old man, surely to have got her pregnant would have been a step in the right direction? But he was afraid that it was so, and that Gently should know it . . . why? Was there something in Hansom's far-fetched notion after all – had the murder of Nicholas Huysmann been the concerted act of his daughter and his chauffeur?

Gretchen, he thought again. Gretchen. Perhaps his best chance lay there. But Gretchen wouldn't talk any more than Fisher . . . and in her present situation, to bring any sort of pressure to bear on her was distasteful. Yet . . . could Hansom have hit it?

The music lilted some far-off tune of Gently's youth, something connected with people and places unspeakably remote. He laid down his knife and fork. The waitress, who had been watching, came forward directly and removed the plate, wondering why Gently shook his head. Several people came in at that moment and stood looking for tables. Secure in his nook, Gently looked them over. Townspeople going to a show and having tea out . . . and then his eyebrows lifted the merest shade. One of the newcomers was Susan.

But Susan was on her own. Also, she seemed to be in a little 'state' about something. She ignored the waitress who wanted to fit her in a large table and with a toss of her sweeping blonde locks made for a smaller one near Gently's own.

'But we are keeping that table for two of our regulars, madam . . .'

'There's no "reserved" notice on it, is there?'

'It is their usual table, madam . . .'

'A pot of tea and some cakes.'

The waitress shrugged and moved away. Gently indulged in a smile. Someone had let Susan down, he thought, she's all dressed up with nowhere to go . . . is Mr Leaming the culprit? He took delivery of his fruit salad and ate it thoughtfully. How much did Susan know about Fisher and Gretchen? She seemed to be a good deal in Gretchen's confidence, one way or another . . . in fact, most of the clandestine comings and goings in the Huysmann house revolved round Susan. Gently eyed her interestedly over his peaches and cherries. She was dressed to go somewhere, without a doubt. She wore a rather expensive black creation that clung to her challengingly, nylons and a red swagger coat which also looked expensive. Her face was made-up heavily but with taste. She wore a silver bracelet, pearls and a diamond ring which might have been genuine. She was quite something, if the sulky expression of her face hadn't spoiled it all.

Gently ate on through his cheese and biscuits and drank his coffee. Why had Leaming turned Susan up – if it was Leaming, and it was unlikely to have been anyone else? Lover's quarrel, perhaps? Susan trying to exceed her market value? Or was it something more interesting and relevant?

He lit his pipe and moved over to Susan's table.

'Good evening, Miss Stibbons. Are you expecting someone?' he asked paternally.

Susan looked up from an eclair. 'Oh! Good evening, Inspector . . . no, I'm not expecting anybody.'

Gently sat down in the vacant chair. 'I like this restaurant,' he said, 'it's comfortable and friendly. Is this your evening off, Miss Stibbons?'

Susan gave a little shrug. 'I get most evenings,' she said.

'You don't know how fortunate you are. In my business we're supposed to be on duty twenty-four hours a day . . . though of course, there'd be a riot if anyone tried to enforce it. But we get enough dumped on us at one time or another. Were you going to the pictures?'

'I *was*,' said Susan, aggrievedly.

'I believe the picture at the Regent is quite good. I heard one of the men talking about it.'

'That's the one I was going to see.'

Gently took out his watch. 'You've still time, if you hurry.'

Susan shrugged again. 'I'm not going, now . . .'

Gently puffed a few smoke-rings. 'I should,' he said. 'It'll cheer you up no end.'

'I don't want to be cheered up.'

'Oh come, now, it can't be so bad as that. What happened, Miss Stibbons?' Gently leaned forward like a tender father preparing to make all well.

'I don't know what happened. It wasn't anything I said.' She looked up at him, her blue eyes charged with injured innocence. 'He just told me he'd finished with me – just like that!'

Gently tut-tutted. 'But there must have been a reason?'

'There wasn't, Inspector, no reason at all. He picked me up like he always does and we came up here to have a drink at Backs. He was quiet-like, but I didn't take much notice – he's often like that.'

'What happened then?'

'When we came out there he suddenly went all stiff – you know – but I hadn't said anything at all! He stood there for a bit by the car and then he suddenly said, "It's been nice knowing you, Susan, but it's all over now. We're through," he said, "this has got to end right here." And then he got in the car and went off, and left me flat!'

Gently shook his head sympathetically. 'Perhaps he didn't mean it. Mr Leaming's got a lot on his mind just now.'

'But he *did* mean it! He knows I wouldn't stand for that sort of treatment – and I'm not going to!' She forked viciously at a meringue.

133

'He may have had an appointment.'

'He didn't say anything about appointments.'

'Well . . . these things happen. I wouldn't take it to heart. There's always someone else round the corner, you know.'

'He may find that out before long.'

Gently smiled encouragingly. 'This business has upset a lot of things, my dear, and affected a lot of people. Take Miss Gretchen, for example.'

Susan mangled a section of meringue and thrust it into her mouth. 'Miss Gretchen's all right,' she said, creamily.

'From a material point of view, I suppose she is.'

'It turned out just right for her. I don't know what she'd have done if it hadn't happened, and that's a fact.'

Gently turned the less-attacked side of the dish of cakes towards the waiting fork. 'How do you mean?' he asked casually.

'Well . . . she was always kept at home . . . she didn't understand.'

'What didn't she understand?'

'You know how it is.'

Gently puffed some smoke at a bulb which gleamed dully behind its mock-parchment. 'In trouble, is she?'

'You'll see, if you're here long enough.'

'How long is that?'

Susan frowned prettily over some green marzipan. ''Bout October, I shouldn't be surprised. Somewhere about then. I warned her, you know, but it was too late then – I didn't know about the first once or twice. After that, of course, there wasn't much point in being careful.'

'Is she really in love with him?'

'What — with Fisher?' Susan sniffed scornfully. 'I shouldn't think so. He goes around with anybody — he tried to get me, but I wasn't having any . . . she was just having him because she couldn't get anybody else.'

'Has this business made any difference?'

'Oh, she won't speak to him now. She won't have anything to do with him. If you ask me, he isn't going to be chauffeur at our place much longer.'

'How does he take it?'

'He doesn't care.'

'I wondered if he'd started getting ideas.'

Susan grinned, cat-like. 'I daresay he had some, but they won't be coming off. Miss Gretchen can pick and choose now . . . even though she is in trouble.'

'Ah well . . . it's a strange world.' Gently thumbed the bowl of his defunct pipe and relit it. 'When was the last time they saw each other?'

'You mean the last time they . . .?' queried Susan innocently.

'Yes.'

'Wednesday.'

'Wednesday, eh?' Gently brooded.

'That's the night Mrs Turner goes to the pictures. She doesn't know anything about it, of course. Miss Gretchen went to bed early and I was there to let him in through the kitchen.'

'Saturday one of his days?'

'Afternoons on a Saturday — I'm out myself after tea.'

'I don't suppose you saw anything of him last Saturday?'

Susan wrinkled her brow. 'I thought maybe he'd slipped in while I was out of the kitchen . . . I felt sure he'd be up there with her. But then, you see, she'd gone out on her own and he stopped at home . . . well, I suppose they had a row. Anyway, she's finished with him now.'

The cakes were finished and the coffee drunk. Susan eased back into her chair and explored her painted lips with the tip of an angelic tongue. 'I like to have a talk,' she said confidentially, 'it makes you feel better.'

Gently said: 'What are you going to do now?'

'Oh . . . I don't know.'

'I was thinking of going to the pictures myself. There's still time.'

Susan unfolded herself another peg and embraced him with a liquid smile. 'I've never been out with a policeman before,' she said.

'It's quite safe,' said Gently.

'We-ell!' She inclined her head coyly.

Poker-faced, Gently paid their two bills and helped Susan on with her flaming red coat. Across the way was a taxi rank. Gently shepherded her through the traffic and handed her into the first car. 'Regent,' he said to the driver, then paused. Over by the Princess foyer stood somebody, watching them, a tall, broad-shouldered figure in an American-cut jacket. Gently shrugged and got in.

'Who was that?' asked Susan.

'Could have been one of our men.'

'I thought it looked like Fisher.'

'Could have been him, too.'

Susan laughed and snuggled against him silkily. 'I've never been out with a policeman before,' she repeated.

★　★　★

At Charlie's the proprietor was in the back helping Elsie with the washing-up. The snack-bar had a sordid, end-of-the-day atmosphere, with dirty cups on the tables and litter on the floor. Its only occupants were the tug-skipper and his mate, who sat talking interminably in low tones, and Fisher, who sat by himself with a cup of tea before him. Outside the street was deserted and silent. Inside there was an occasional clink of cup and saucer from the back and the drone of the conversation, on and on, like an audition from another world. A coffee-stained evening paper carrying Peter Huysmann's photograph shared a table with a half-eaten bun.

Fisher played with the spoon in his saucer. His mouth was small and tight, his dark eyes angry and furtive. They glanced at the two tug-men, at the door, at the clock, which showed eleven. He pulled over the paper, limp and dirty, and stared at it. Why had Charlie looked at him like that when he came in? Why had he said: 'What – *you*?' in that sort of way? Charlie was in with the police, he knew that. Suppose they'd dropped something to him – something about Fisher? But he was safe there, as long as he kept his trap shut . . . they might suspect, but they couldn't prove anything.

Fisher crumpled the paper and threw it into a corner, done and finished with. He looked across at the two tug-men. They were completely absorbed in their conversation . . . or was it that they didn't want to speak to him? Had Charlie said something to them? He could imagine Charlie bending over and whispering: 'Stay clear of Fisher – the police have got something on him!' And so they talked and talked and pretended he wasn't there. He got up and went over to them. They stopped talking and looked round. A movement from the back suggested that Charlie had put his head round the door.

'I'm Fisher,' he said defiantly.

The tug-skipper shrugged his lean shoulders. 'What about it, mate?' he retorted.

'I'm Huysmann's chauffeur.'

'Well . . . what are we supposed to do . . . clap?'

'I could tell them a few things they don't know, if I'd a mind to . . . things they're never going to find out without me.'

Charlie said from the door: 'Well – why don't you tell them? What are you afraid of?'

Fisher swung round to face him. 'I'm not afraid of nothing – see? They can't pin anything on me, whatever they think – and whatever they say they think!'

'What do they think, mate?' put in the tug-skipper.

'Never you mind . . . it isn't your business.'

'Then why come barging in with it?'

Fisher clenched his fists and looked ugly. 'Here . . . stop that!' exclaimed Charlie, coming round from behind the bar.

'Let him be,' said the tug-skipper, 'I know how to handle his type . . .'

'I won't have fighting here.'

Fisher turned furiously on Charlie. 'Policeman!' he burst out, 'bloody policeman! I'm not a policeman, whatever else I am. And you watch out for yourself, that's what I say. Things are going to change round here . . . you may not be so high and mighty, for one!'

Charlie took him by the sleeve. 'What do you mean by that?' he demanded.

'Get your hands off me – get them off!'

'I'm asking you what you mean by what you just said.'

Fisher wrenched himself away. 'You'll find out, don't worry! You'll find out that you can't treat some people like dirt . . .!'

The doorbell tinkled and the bulky figure of Gently entered. He glanced at Fisher with mild surprise. 'We seem to be following each other about . . .' he said.

'Rotten cop!' shouted Fisher, 'coming here trying to find out things . . . but there's nothing you can find out. Ask your pal Charlie, here!'

Gently ignored him and went over to the counter. 'A cup of coffee,' he said. Charlie, with a dangerous glance at Fisher, went to serve him. 'Look at him!' cried Fisher, trying to include the tug-men, 'a bloody know-all cop! A rotten sneaking policeman! Treating us as though we were something out of a drain!'

The second tug-man shifted uneasily. 'If he's a policeman you'd better button your mouth up, chum,' he said. But Fisher would not be silenced. 'You'd think he was clever to look at him – he thinks he's clever himself! But he isn't – not really! There's as clever people as he is about and they aren't chief inspectors . . .' Encouraged by Gently's passive acceptance of his taunts, Fisher moved closer to the counter. 'You took Susan to the pictures, didn't you? I know – I was watching you! And what did you get out of her, I'd like to know? How much do you think she knows?'

Gently turned about and surveyed him expression-lessly. 'Why did Leaming turn her up tonight?' he asked.

'Leaming!' Fisher spat on the floor. 'How should I know why he did it? What's it got to do with me?'

'I was just asking . . .' replied Gently smoothly.

'Bloody coppers – always asking questions! But you won't get anything out of me. And if you've got any sense you won't listen to Susan's lies . . . dirty little bitch!'

Gently turned his back and stirred his coffee. Charlie looked at him questioningly, but Gently's lips framed a negative.

'What's she been saying about me?' blustered Fisher, pushing up and trying to make Gently look at him. 'She's been lying . . . I've a right to know!'

Gently placed his spoon in the saucer and drank some coffee.

'If it's anything about me and Gretchen, it's a bloody lie!'

Gently put his cup down.

'Listen!' shouted Fisher, 'I've got a right to know – you're going to tell me!' and he laid his hand on Gently's shoulder. He didn't realize how big a mistake this was . . .

Unfortunately, the memory of a fragment of masonry bouncing along the pavement came into Gently's mind at the critical moment and he put plenty of pull into the movement. Fisher lay on his back, completely stunned.

'My God!' exclaimed the tug-skipper, 'I didn't even see it happen!'

Gently dusted his hands modestly. 'It's something they teach you at police college . . .' he said. He motioned to Charlie. 'Put him outside while he's quiet.' He looked at the two tug-men thoughtfully. 'I saw you come up this morning. You dropped a barge at the other side of Railway Bridge. Who was that for?' he enquired.

The two tug-men looked at each other and the skipper ran his tongue over his lips. 'It was sawn-out stuff – we drop it there to save time,' he said.

'Does that quay belong to Huysmann's?'

'Well, no . . . it don't. But they handle the stuff there for us.'

'Who handles it?'

'I reckon it's the firm we supply it to.'

'And who are they?'

The skipper paused reluctantly, then shrugged his shoulders. 'They call themselves "The Straight Grain Timber Merchants".'

Gently smiled at the distant reaches of the night. 'It's the first time I've heard of that particular firm,' he said.

CHAPTER TEN

T HE HUYSMANN AFFAIR had turned stale by Tuesday. The fun and games were over with the arrest of Peter and although the failure to charge him with the murder was still good for a minor headline, feeling was that time would take care of that . . . as, indeed, it would. More current now was the pulled muscle of the City's centre-forward. The situation was very keen at the top of the third division south.

Impatient Hansom, having slept on it, ventured a suggestion that the super should reverse his decision and charge Peter forthwith. It was Hansom's first chance of getting an unaided homicide conviction . . . it might easily be his last. But the super, also having slept on it, was convinced that his decision had been wise. He had known Gently longer than had Hansom. He had also begun to be affected by a little of Gently's doubt about the case. So he trailed a convenient smoke-screen before the powers that be and went about his superintendental duties with a thoughtful mien.

Mrs Peter Huysmann had seen her husband at police headquarters. In the presence of a curious constable there had been very little said on either side. Such hopes as had been raised in Mrs Huysmann by the delay in charging Peter were quickly shaken – Peter himself had very few. 'But it must mean something . . .' she said. He shook his head. 'It means they're waiting until they've got everything ready.' 'But did you see Chief Inspector Gently, Peter? He *knows* you didn't do it . . . he told me so!' 'He doesn't belong here. Cathy, it won't make any difference.'

'Fancy!' said Mrs Turner to Susan, 'going out with a policeman – and that one too, who's old enough to be your grandfather! I knew you weren't particular, my girl, but I didn't know you'd come as low as that.' Susan sniffed infuriatingly. 'He's a nice man,' she said, 'I like him . . . he's got good taste.' 'He must have been after something or he wouldn't have taken you out!' 'You're completely wrong,' said Susan, 'he wasn't after anything. He was just being sympathetic and nice and manny . . .'

Gretchen's bedroom was small, almost an attic, with a narrow window looking across the river to the willow trees down Riverside. The floor was stained and naked; the walls, distempered grey, bore nothing but a carved wood crucifix and a narrow iron bed, a white-painted deal wash-stand and a cane-bottom chair comprised all the furniture. Gretchen knelt for long periods on the bare floor in front of the crucifix. Her lips murmured over and over: O my God, I am sorry for my sins . . . let me be forgiven and show me the way.

There came a tap at the bolted door. 'Just a minute!' Gretchen called, and rose, rubbing her painful knees. At the door was Susan. 'It's the Chief Inspector, miss – he

143

wants to know if you can see him.' Gretchen hesitated. 'Which – which one is the Chief Inspector?' 'He's the one from Scotland Yard, miss . . . the quiet one who's always nice to you.' 'Very well . . . tell him that I shall be down directly.'

Susan went, and Gretchen moved across to the white-painted wash-stand, which had a small mirror. She patted her straight black hair with plump fingers, turned sideways and examined herself critically. Then she looked back into her dark eyes, large, heavy, betraying nothing except that they had something to betray.

Gently was waiting in the hall. He came forward, smiling sunnily, and took her plump, limp hand. 'I hope I haven't broken in on you too early,' he said. Gretchen shook her neat head. 'I am usually up at six o'clock . . . we have always been early risers.'

Gently said: 'I'd like to have a little chat in the study, if you are agreeable.'

'In the study?' She looked at him in some dismay.

'I want to glance through the papers in your father's desk . . . of course, we can talk elsewhere if you prefer it. I only wanted to kill two birds with one stone.'

Gretchen took two quick little breaths. 'It does not matter . . . one must grow used to these things.' Gently led the way to the study.

The study had a forlorn, removed look, shaken out of its familiar self by the absence of the carpet, which the local police had taken away, and the slight redistribution of the furniture which this had occasioned. Gently dusted off a chair with his handkerchief and placed it for Gretchen. He himself sat down at the desk and began a leisurely examination of the contents of the drawers.

'Your brother is bearing up well,' he observed, aside. 'I asked him if he had any message for you, and he said to tell you that you mustn't worry, because somehow it would come out what really happened.'

Gretchen said: 'I would like to see him, when I may.'

Gently nodded, peering into a file of advice notes. 'There won't be any difficulty made about that. You can come along with me, if you like. I suppose you didn't know much about your father's business affairs, my dear?'

'Oh no . . . he did not think that a woman had any part in business.'

'He was one of the old school . . . I'm just a child at business matters myself. I spent a couple of hours looking through the firm's books on Sunday, but I might just as well have had a nap. Why doesn't somebody think out a way of making book-keeping intelligible?'

Gretchen kept her dark eyes riveted upon him, on edge, trying to gather something of what would come. But Gently seemed to be in no hurry. He prodded and poked, drawer by drawer, sometimes musing over bits and pieces with raised eyebrows, as though he had forgotten Gretchen's existence. Occasionally he made a remark of no particular significance and once or twice he asked questions about things. For the rest, Gretchen might just as well not have been there and towards the end of Gently's investigating she began to get impatient.

At last he appeared to have finished. He replaced everything which had been removed except a green card and closed the drawers. The card he handed to Gretchen. 'Have you seen this before?' he asked.

She nodded. 'It is an advice card from his suppliers in Holland . . . this is perhaps the last one.'

'Do you remember it being received?'

'I think it came one day my father went to London on business. He picked up his mail as he went out.'

'There is something scribbled across one of the margins. Would that be your father's handwriting?'

'Oh yes. He often made little notes like this.'

'Have you ever heard that name before – "The Straight Grain Timber Merchants"?'

'I know nothing of his business . . .'

'The name is entirely unfamiliar to you?'

'Yes . . . entirely unfamiliar.'

Gently received back the card and put it carefully away in his wallet. He took out a large new bag of peppermint creams. 'Have one?' he invited. Gretchen refused. Gently placed half a dozen of them on the desk in line-of-battle and stowed the bag back in his pocket again.

He said: 'Miss Gretchen, I think it's time you told me the truth about last Saturday.'

Gretchen started back in her chair. 'Inspector . . . what is it you mean? I've told you everything!'

Gently shook his head sadly and removed the first of the peppermint creams. He said nothing.

'But you took it down . . . everything I said! What more can there be?'

'First,' said Gently, swallowing, 'you didn't go to the pictures, Miss Gretchen.'

'But I did . . . to the Carlton . . . it was *Meet Me in Rio*!'

'Secondly,' continued Gently, unheeding, 'the chauffeur, Fisher, was in the habit of visiting you on Saturday afternoons, here, in this house.'

'You cannot say that, oh no . . .!'

'And thirdly,' proceeded Gently, 'Fisher did not spend

146

the afternoon at his flat, as he would have us believe. He left it at about two o'clock and returned again at four twenty-two and a half p.m. exactly. In addition to this somebody – and I suggest it was either Fisher or yourself – was seen by your brother at the head of the main stairway when he entered.'

'But this is . . . impossible!'

'There are supplementary facts, Miss Gretchen. Fisher has been your lover since January. You are with child by Fisher. You have refused to see Fisher since the discovery of the crime. Fisher has been hinting that he may soon be boss here. He has also hinted that he has knowledge of the crime unknown to the police. When you have added all that together, Miss Gretchen, you will come to the irresistible conclusion that both you and he spent the Saturday afternoon in this house.'

Gretchen gave a low moan and buried her face in her two plump hands.

'I can appreciate your feelings,' said Gently kindly, 'and believe me, I hate this side of the business almost as much as yourself. But there are some important things which must take the place of personal considerations or there could be no human society. Miss Gretchen, if your brother is to receive justice you must tell the truth. His life is very nearly in your hands.'

'It isn't true,' moaned Gretchen, 'I can't help him . . . it isn't true!' and her shoulders heaved with sobbing.

Gently took the second peppermint cream. 'If you won't speak,' he said, 'you are leaving me with only one possible conclusion. I shall have to think that you are shielding your lover at the expense of your brother's life and that you are doing it because you can only save his life by accusing your lover . . . is that what you want me to think?'

Gretchen sprang upright, staring at him. 'No, no! That is not so – he didn't do it!'

'But what else can I think, if you will not tell me the truth?'

'I tell you he did not do it!'

Gently shrugged and shook his head, made a pattern with the four remaining peppermint creams. Into the comparative quiet of the room broke the distant shriek of a circular saw biting at oak. The sound was mirrored by a quiver that ran through Gretchen's body. 'Look!' she said, 'I tell you – I tell you the truth about myself!'

Gently's eyebrows lifted slightly. 'I would like the truth about everything you can tell me, Miss Gretchen.'

'It is about everything . . . it is the truth . . .' She stared at him with wide open eyes, as though she would compel him to believe her by the naked will. 'You are right, I did not go to the pictures . . . at least, I did not go in. I just go there to find out about it so I can pretend, that is all.'

'At what time was this, Miss Gretchen?'

'I don't know . . . about half-past four.'

'It would be about the time that Fisher returned to his flat . . . or a little longer, to enable you to reach the Carlton?'

'He – was – not – there!' She beat on her knees with her clenched hands. 'I do not know where he is – if he go out, he go out, but it is not to me. I am the one who was there, in the house . . . it is me that Peter sees . . .'

'Just a moment,' Gently interrupted, 'let's begin at the beginning, shall we? What did you do after lunch?'

'I told you, I have a wash, then I fetch my coffee from the kitchen and take it to my room.'

'Was Susan in the kitchen when you fetched your coffee?'

'But of course.'

'Did you have any conversation with Susan at that time?'

'No doubt . . . we said something.'

'Did she ask you, for instance, whether you were expecting a visit from Fisher that afternoon?'

'It may be that she did.'

'And what did you reply?'

'Oh . . . nothing special. I just shrug my shoulders and let her think what she like.'

'You gave her the impression that he was coming?'

'I do not know.'

'It was the afternoon on which he customarily visited you, Miss Gretchen. If you gave Susan the impression that he was not coming, then surely she would have commented on it and perhaps enquired why that was so. Did she do this?'

'No . . . I think perhaps she thought he was coming.'

'Why was it, in fact, that he did not come?'

Gretchen twisted her hands together. 'How should I know . . .?'

'Then you were expecting him?'

'No! I knew he would not come . . . I think he told me that the last time, but I forget why.'

'Had there been a quarrel?'

'Perhaps it was that.'

'Had it come to your knowledge that Fisher associated with other women besides yourself?'

The clenched hands pulled apart. 'I do not know that!'

'Then why did you quarrel?'

'Perhaps it was not a quarrel. Maybe I told him it was too dangerous for him to keep coming like that.'

'And he agreed straight away not to come any more?'

'Well . . . he agreed.'

'Had you some reason why it should be more dangerous than it had been in the past?'

'I don't know . . . it was never safe that he should come.'

'And he was quite agreeable to give it up immediately on your suggestion?'

'. . . yes!'

Gently picked up the third peppermint cream and ate it solemnly. 'Miss Gretchen,' he said, 'would you consider it as being an unusual coincidence that this should happen immediately before your father was murdered?'

Gretchen bit her lip, but said nothing. Gently swallowed the peppermint cream and arranged the remaining three in a triangle. 'Ah well . . .' he sighed, 'you took your coffee to your room. What did you do then?'

'I . . . prayed.'

'And how long were you occupied with prayer?'

'That I do not know. Sometimes one is taken away and the prayer is very long. It may have been an hour, or less.'

'You would not be aware of anything that was taking place in the house while you were praying?'

'Oh no! I am not in the house, then. It is like a far country where everything is . . . changed.'

'And you do not know precisely when your praying ended?'

'I think it was when Peter came. I heard him and got up.'

'But you have just said that you would not have been

150

aware of anything which was taking place in the house while you were praying, Miss Gretchen.'

The hands twisted again, finger over finger. 'Perhaps I got up before that . . . just before.'

'And then you came out on the landing to see if it was Peter?'

'I thought it would be him . . . I did not know.'

'He says that you withdrew immediately he looked towards you. Why was that?'

'Oh . . . my father would have been angry . . . he might have come out to see who it was.'

'But surely there was no need to have hidden away from him – you might have smiled to him or greeted him with a few words from the landing and still have been in a position to withdraw if your father should have appeared?'

'I don't know . . . I thought it was best not to see him.'

'Tell me what happened after that.'

'I stayed up there on the landing to hear how my father would receive Peter. At first I heard nothing, but later on they raised their voices and I knew it was not going well for him. I heard Peter call my father some names and my father say things which I could not make out. So I crept down the stairs and along the passage in order to hear them better.'

'Between the time when Peter went in and the time when you went down, did you see anybody in the hall?'

'There was nobody there.'

'You're quite sure of that?'

'Oh yes.'

'Then you did not see Susan pass through from the dining-room to the kitchen?'

'Susan? Of course! I thought you meant somebody else . . .'

'Continue with your account, please.'

'I could not hear anything when I went down the stairs . . . they had stopped talking. I stood close to the door, but they had finished, so I thought that Peter must have gone. I was just going to go back again, then . . .'

Gretchen broke off, shaking her head stupidly.

'Then?' prompted Gently.

'. . . then I heard my father . . . scream.'

'What sort of scream?'

'Oh, dreadful . . . terrible! . . . as one screams at a terrible injury . . .'

'What did you do?'

Her head continued to shake, senselessly, like the head of a mechanical doll. 'I stood still . . . I daren't move . . . I could not move at all. I don't know how long it was that I was like that.'

'But afterwards?'

'Afterwards . . . I got the door open and he lay there with the knife in his back . . . by the safe, where you found him.'

Gently said: 'Nobody had passed you in the passage and there was nobody else in the study . . . is that so?'

'Yes . . . nobody.'

'And you heard no movements that suggested the presence of some other person?'

'I heard movements in the study directly after the scream, but nothing else.'

'What sort of movements?'

'First, a thud . . . then the safe door, which squeaks . . . after that it was somebody moving across the room.'

'Nothing else?'

'No.'

'Not after you had entered the study?'

'I heard nothing then . . . I was not listening.'

'What did you do?'

Gretchen spread her hands over her knees and took a deep breath. 'I went and got the knife,' she said.

'What was your object?'

'It was a throwing knife, and Peter could throw knives . . . also, it would have his fingerprints on it.'

'Did you notice if the side door was open?'

'Yes, it was.'

'And the garden gate?'

'I did not notice that.'

'What did you do when you had got the knife?'

'I wiped the handle of it with the hem of my skirt and hid it in the chest . . . then I went up to my room again. All the time it was quiet, there was no sign of Susan. I say to myself: "She does not know if I am here or if I am not, and I could easily have slipped out earlier on . . . if she sees me come in, she will believe it when I say I went out after lunch." So I put on my coat and creep out through the study. Then of course I went up to the Carlton to find out everything that was on . . . I came back a little while after Mrs Turner.'

Gently removed another peppermint cream from his shrinking battalion. 'Doesn't it occur to you, Miss Gretchen,' he said, 'that it would have been considerably wiser to have left the knife where it was, and to have phoned the police immediately?'

Gretchen stared at him with wide-open eyes. 'But my brother . . . I had to do something to help him!'

153

'And what in effect did you do?' asked Gently. 'Your brother was bound to be the principal suspect, with or without the knife. Furthermore, the prints on the knife may not have been his. Didn't that occur to you, Miss Gretchen?'

'I don't know . . . I didn't think . . .'

'In which case you will have destroyed the one piece of evidence which would have cleared your brother on the spot. But apart from that, why did you take the trouble of establishing an alibi for yourself? It hardly seems worth the trouble. Once you had satisfied yourself about the knife there was no reason why you should not have contacted the police . . . at least, nothing that appears in the account you have given.'

'My brother . . . it give him time to get away.'

'What connection is there between that and your alibi? Why did you *want* an alibi, Miss Gretchen? It was a difficult thing to establish and it was bound to bring suspicion on you . . . quite unnecessarily, by your account.'

Gretchen twisted herself in her chair. 'I just think it best if you think I have nothing to do with it . . .'

Gently shook his head. 'It doesn't seem worthwhile to me. People in murder cases who can prove their innocence are usually very keen to tell the truth.'

'But it was as I say!'

'It was not to shield someone other than your brother?'

'No!'

'It was not because Fisher was with you?'

'I tell you he is not!'

'Not because he might be suspected of having been here, unless you could prove you were somewhere else?'

154

Gretchen covered her face with her hands again and sobbed.

'And not,' continued Gently remorselessly, 'because you knew him to be the murderer?'

'No, no! It is not so! Oh why are you asking these things . . . why . . . why . . .?'

Gently sighed and reached for the penultimate peppermint cream. The saws in the yard screamed savagely, two, three, four of them. In his mind's eye Gently saw the blades tearing into the ponderous trunks, cruel and merciless, ripping them into the geometrical shapes of man.

'Do you intend to marry Fisher?' he asked.

Gretchen sobbed on.

'I understand that you have been refusing to see him.'

She looked at him for a moment, tear-wet. 'I shall not see him any more.'

Gently shrugged. 'I don't blame you,' he said, 'he's not the sort of man to make a good husband . . .'

Gretchen sobbed.

'Still, I'm surprised to find him thrown over so quickly.'

'It is to do with me!' she burst out. 'Why have I to tell you about this? Leave me alone!'

'I was wondering if it had to do with me.'

'I tell you nothing more . . . nothing more at all!'

Gently rose, went over to the small window and stood for a moment looking out at the neat little garden with its high walls and quaint summer-house. 'You haven't told me the truth, Miss Gretchen,' he said.

There was no answer but her sobbing.

'I'm going now, but I shall be coming back. In the meantime I would like you to think over your situation

155

very, very seriously.' He moved back into the room. 'Your brother's life is in danger and it may be only by your telling us everything you know that his innocence can be established. I want you to think about that during the next few hours.'

She looked up suddenly. 'I'd like to . . .' she began, her hands gripping each other convulsively.

'Yes . . .?'

'Please, I'd like to . . .' She broke off as a brisk tap sounded at the door. Gently's lips compressed and he strode across and opened it. Leaming stood in the doorway.

'Hullo, Inspector!' he said, 'I didn't realize you were here . . . I've come to fetch a check-list.' He glanced at Gretchen in surprise. 'Why, Miss Huysmann . . . you've been crying!' he said.

CHAPTER ELEVEN

LEAMING'S VERMILION PASHLEY slid out of the yard with a surge of conscious power and rode superbly down Queen Street towards Railway Bridge. Gently adjusted himself in the well-padded seat and lit a hand-made cigarette. 'I hope your housekeeper isn't going to mind my coming to lunch . . .' he said. Leaming smiled handsomely. 'Don't worry about that. She always cooks for half a dozen.' 'If I took home someone on spec my housekeeper would go on strike . . .'

The Pashley swept over the bridge and into Railway Road. On the right reared the long, high, windowless back of the football-ground stands. Leaming indicated it with a movement of his head. 'That's it,' he said, 'one of the best grounds outside the First Division. They've got another home match on Saturday . . . the Cobblers . . . usually a hard game. Going to see them?'

'I might,' said Gently. 'Are you?'

Leaming made a face. 'This business is meaning a lot of extra work . . . we've got the accountants in next week. I shall have to spend the weekend preparing for them.'

'You'll have to make sure of your pink'un.'

Leaming dashed away some cigarette ash and was silent. The Pashley sped on through the narrow, smoke-visaged streets adjacent to the marshalling yards and out to the east-bound road. Here it went through Earton, a residential suburb built round a village, and the narrow, twisted road packed with traffic gave Leaming plenty of opportunity to display both his car and his skill. They passed Earton Green, a narrow, tree-shaded strip bounded by the Yar, where rivercraft, spick and span from their winter grooming, lay fresh-launched and naked at boat-yard quays. Past the Green the road widened, still going through suburbs, hesitating before it shook off the last straggling cottages and plunged into the country beyond.

Here Leaming gunned the Pashley till it was leaping eastwards in the eighties. He would probably have gone faster, but the road wasn't built for really high speeds and there was a good deal of outgoing traffic to be passed.

'Like it?' he jerked at Gently.

'Not really,' admitted Gently frankly.

'I can get a hundred and fifteen out of her on the Newmarket road – going down to London I reached Hatfield one hour dead out of Norchester.'

'You must miss an awful lot that way.'

'I've missed everything so far!'

Gently's ordeal did not last long. Three miles beyond Norchester they came to the side turning which led to Haswick. Monk's Thatch, Leaming's house, stood at the nearer end. It was a beautiful modern riverside dwelling standing amongst trees, hidden from the road by a shrubbery. The verandaed front looked over a terraced lawn to the river and a thatched boat-house, standing apart, suggested that Leaming had other interests as well as cars.

Gently said: 'All this must have cost you a penny.'

Leaming shrugged. 'My father left me a little money, you know . . .'

He led the way into the house and showed Gently where he could wash. The indoor appointments matched the outdoor ones in opulence. By the time he was sat down to lunch on a Chippendale dining-room chair, one of a suite, Gently had formed quite a respect for Leaming's father.

Leaming said: 'Of course, you must have guessed that I had a double motive in asking you to lunch. I very much want to hear what's happening with young Peter.'

'Ah . . .!' Gently said, and helped himself to new potatoes.

'I was flabbergasted when he wasn't charged. It seemed more than we could hope for . . . at the same time, it set me wondering what was at the back of it.'

Gently crunched a piece of pork crackling. 'Just means there's some doubt,' he said.

'You mean you're on to something else?'

'Could mean that.'

'And is it likely that young Peter will be cleared, without it ever going into court?'

'That depends on a lot of things.'

'But there's a good chance of that? I know I'm asking you rather a lot, Inspector, but you can't know how much this business means to me. Peter has been – well, almost a nephew to me, if you can understand that, and I've committed myself to stand by him now, whatever the cost. So if you can give me a little information – strictly off the record – I shall be extremely grateful.' He glanced at Gently winningly.

Gently laid down his knife and took a thoughtful mouthful of beer. 'There's a lot of things to be cleared up,' he said. 'Until they are, I wouldn't be too hopeful.'

'Is Fisher one of those things?'

'I think Fisher could give us some interesting information, if he had a mind to.'

'You know, Inspector, if I had to put my finger on one particular person and say "that's him", I should put it on Fisher.'

'You would?' mused Gently.

'Yes, I would.'

'Have you any especial reason for saying that?'

'He just seems to me the one person who would do it. Isn't that your opinion?'

Gently drank some more beer. 'I suppose he's quite a likely customer,' he said.

'Ah! I thought you would agree.' Leaming returned to his plate for a moment, then said, through the tail-end of a mouthful: 'I believe there's something in that business about him and Gretchen, after all.'

Gently elevated an eyebrow.

'Yes, I know I pooh-poohed it when you suggested it the other day, but I've heard a bit of gossip about it since then.'

'Where?' said Gently, eating.

'I was in that snack-bar across the street from the yard – I heard it mentioned there. Quite confidently, you know, as though there was no doubt about it.'

'Could be just gossip,' said Gently.

'You think there's nothing in it? But there could be some connection there, when you think about it. Just suppose he'd got her into trouble . . . they'd be in a mess, wouldn't they? Both of them . . .'

'You've got a theory about that . . .?'

'Well . . . somebody did the old man in . . . and there must have been a reason for it.'

'Yes, there must have been a reason . . .'

'Of course, there's the money to think of. If Fisher did for the old man with the idea of clearing the way to marry Gretchen, there'd be no point in his pinching it.'

'There's a great temptation in ready money.'

'You're right, of course . . . do you think he did it?'

Gently smiled at the river-side willows. 'I may have an answer to that one shortly.'

Leaming ate and was silent for a short spell. Gently plied himself appreciatively with pork, and added a few more potatoes to his plate . . . after all, what does one's figure matter when one is the wrong side of fifty?

Leaming said: 'When I was talking to you about the money turning up, I didn't know that one note was going to turn up so quickly . . . and right in the wrong place, too.'

Gently said: 'Mmp.'

'But it's still a good angle, don't you think? That money's got to turn up some time.'

'It's not all that easy to trace when it does turn up . . . it may have gone through a lot of hands.'

'There's that, of course . . . but once it starts turning up you're pretty sure that Peter's in the clear.'

'Could be,' said Gently.

Leaming laughed. 'For all I know, of course, that's what's happened . . . maybe that's why Peter wasn't charged. Well, if that's the case, you may well say you'll have an answer shortly.' He glanced at Gently interrogatively.

'And if, in addition, someone cracked . . .'

'You mean Fisher?'

'Perhaps.'

Leaming went back to his eating.

Gently said: 'There's a time in every case that I've had anything to do with when you suddenly find yourself over the top of the hill . . . usually, there's no good reason for it. You just keep pushing and pushing, never seeming to get anywhere, and then some time you find you don't have to push any longer . . . the thing you've been pushing starts to carry you along with it. It's odd, isn't it?'

Leaming said: 'And you've reached that stage in this case?'

Gently shrugged. 'I've got that feeling . . .'

Leaming studied his plate without expression, making small, deliberate movements with his knife. Gently chewed a piece of roll and washed it down with beer. Across the lawn he could see a dinghy, a class-boat, tacking wistfully against the tide, long, painfully slow tacks amongst the trees, with scarcely enough breeze to give it headway. Back and forth it went, its helmsman, patient and determined, moving across with each new tack . . . it seemed like a machine which had lost its raison d'être, still obstinately performing its functions but going nowhere. Gently returned his eyes to the table and found that Leaming was staring at him.

'You do any sailing?' asked Gently.

'I've got a one-design in the boat-house.'

'What do they fetch these days?'

'You might pick one up for two-fifty.'

'That lets me out . . . I'm only a policeman.'

The housekeeper took their plates and served the

sweet, which was rhubarb pie and cream. Gently went to work with unabated gusto. 'You've a good cook,' he said, between mouthfuls. Leaming smiled and picked up his fork and spoon. 'I have to do entertaining sometimes . . .'

The dinghy had made the next bend at last and Gently, outside the rhubarb and cream, was looking round for the coffee coming in. 'By the way,' he said, licking his lips, 'I knew there was something I meant to ask you about . . .' He got out his wallet and extracted the green card from it. 'Know anything about these people?' he asked.

Leaming took the card while Gently made room for his cup of coffee. 'That's Huysmann's writing . . .' said Leaming. Gently took three lumps of sugar and began stirring them. The housekeeper retired with her tray.

'I found it in Huysmann's desk this morning,' said Gently helpfully. 'I thought I'd heard the name before somewhere . . .'

Leaming looked from the card to Gently and back at the card again. Then he turned the card over and appeared to study the verso. Gently seemed not to watch him.

'It's one of his notes all right,' said Leaming at length, 'he was for ever scribbling things down . . .'

Gently took it back from him. 'Miss Gretchen verified the handwriting . . . it is the firm I should like to know about.'

Leaming eyed him intently. 'It's a firm we do business with,' he said evenly.

'What sort of business?'

'We supply them with sawn-out timber.'

'And have you been connected with them very long?'

'Oh . . . quite a few years.'

'Ten years, say?'

'Not so long as that.'

Gently reinserted the card in his wallet and tucked it into his pocket. 'I wonder why Mr Huysmann made a note of the firm's name . . . as though it were unfamiliar?' he pondered.

Leaming shrugged slightly. 'It may have been to jog his memory about a contract.'

'But why write out the name in full? . . . Also, I don't remember coming across it when I went through the books.'

Leaming stared straight ahead of him. 'We keep separate books for that firm,' he said.

'Separate books? Why is that?'

'We supply them with sawn-out stuff that hasn't been through the mill . . . we simply act as middlemen. The stuff is processed at Starmouth and we bring it up for them. We take about fifteen per cent on it.'

'Isn't it unusual for a milling firm to supply timber which has been milled elsewhere? I should have thought it would have been more profitable to have supplied timber from one's own mill.'

'You have to do it sometimes, when the mill is working at capacity.'

'But this has been going on over a number of years.'

Leaming bit his lip. 'I imagine Huysmann is the only one who could give you an answer to that . . . and he won't answer any more questions.'

'I thought that perhaps his manager could have told me.' Gently drank his coffee, looking at Leaming across the cup. 'It's an interesting problem . . . I should like to know more about it. Have you got these people's address?'

'Actually, I don't think we have.'

Gently's eyebrows lifted. 'But surely you must have . . .?'

'No.' Leaming put down his cup and faced Gently. 'You see, Inspector, they pay cash on delivery. We simply bring the wood up and they collect it and pay. And that's all we know about them.'

Gently shook his head puzzledly. 'I never did know much about business . . .' he said. 'All the same, I'd like to look over the books. Was it a very large turnover?'

'About twelve thousand a year . . . but we only took fifteen per cent on that.'

Leaming rose, producing his gold cigarette case as he did so. Gently accepted a cigarette. 'I shall have to be getting back,' Leaming said, 'sorry if I have to rush you.' Gently followed him out to the Pashley and settled his bulky figure in the seat. 'It was a very good lunch . . . you must ask me again some time.' Leaming smiled automatically and sent the Pashley bounding down the drive. 'I like having a chat over lunch,' he said, 'I think it helps to keep you in perspective . . . don't you?'

Queen Street was somnolent in a warm afternoon. The mild, sun-in-cloud sky produced no shadows, only a pervading brightness, and the few vehicles making their way to and from the city seemed to move drowsily, as though the machines themselves were infected by the atmosphere. Even the sawmill seemed subdued, and the bundling and clanking noises from the breweries sounded sleepy and far away. Gently stood on the pavement feeling stupid. He had overeaten rather at lunch.

He pulled himself together and went into Charlie's.

Two of the inevitable transport drivers sat at a table eating rolls and drinking tea, one of them wearily turning the pages of a ragged *Picture Post*. The girl Elsie was at the counter. She sniffed as Gently entered and poked her head round the curtain, then disappeared through it. A moment later, Charlie himself came out.

'I was hoping you'd look in,' he said, a gleam of satisfaction in his eye.

'You've got something to tell me?'

'Something what happened about half an hour ago.' He darted a quick glance at the two transport drivers and another at Gently. Gently leaned across the zinc-topped counter. 'He was in here having his lunch,' proceeded Charlie in a lowered tone, 'and he'd got the girl Susan with him – right friendly they was together – having a long talk about something or other . . . they was over there in the corner.'

Gently leaned forward a little further.

'I brought their stuff out for them, and I got to hear a little bit of what they was saying. It was about you asking Miss Gretchen questions, Inspector, how you'd been there a long time this morning, and how she'd listened to it and how it was all about Mr Fisher. And they was that friendly together, you'd hardly believe it. He give her some sort of trinket – a bracelet, I think it was, anyway it was something what pleased her – and when I take their tea over, I heard him arranging to take her out.'

Gently's lips formed a soundless whistle. 'You're sure about that?'

'Heard it with my own ears!'

'And she agreed?'

'That she did, first time of asking.'

Gently slowly shook his head. 'Fisher seems to have got a very long way in a very short time . . . a very long way.'

'That's how it struck me, sir. And I couldn't help bringing to mind how he's been talking this last day or two about how things was going to change and all that. Well, they seem to have changed now all right, and that's a fact.'

Gently said: 'There's only one thing that has any weight with Susan . . .'

'But that isn't all, sir. Fisher, he come back here a few minutes later, seems like he was looking for somebody. "What've you lost?" I say, a bit sharp-like. "Never you mind," he say, "but if that b— Inspector Gently comes snooping around here, just you tell him I want to see him, see?" And out he stalks again. So what do you make of that?'

Gently shook his head again. 'He didn't say where I could find him, I suppose?'

'Well, no, he didn't . . .'

'Never mind, Charlie – you're doing well. Keep your eye on him.'

Gently went out of Charlie's with slightly more zest than when he had entered it. Things were undoubtedly whipping up a bit, he told himself. Something was beginning to move . . . He glanced up and down Queen Street for a sight of the familiar figure in the American-style jacket, then ambled slowly away in the direction of the city. At Mariner's Lane he came to a standstill. Had Fisher gone back to his flat? But it was a long climb up there . . . and Gently had overeaten at lunch. Moreover, he could still see the fragment of masonry lying at the side of the pavement where he had placed it . . . and Fisher might be quieter when he dropped the next piece. So Gently continued to promenade along Queen Street.

He passed the Huysmann house, aloof and withdrawn, its great street-ward gables almost windowless, wended round thick-legged women pushing decrepit prams, stopped to light his pipe in a yard-way. He had just completed this operation when the American-style jacket loomed up beside him. He turned his head in mild surprise. 'You do it better than a policeman . . .' he said.

Fisher's dark eyes glared at him. 'You been looking for me?' he asked smoulderingly.

'I thought you were looking for me,' said Gently.

'I got something to say to you.'

'So I gathered, one way or another.'

Fisher indicated the yard from which he had emerged. 'Come up here, Mr Inspector Gently . . . I'm not telling it to half Norchester.'

Gently moved into the derelict yard, glancing round quickly at the disintegrating walls, at rotted flooring from which the nettles sprang, at falling plaster chalked on by children. Fisher sneered: 'You don't need to be afraid . . . nobody's going to jump on you.' Gently shrugged and puffed complacently at his pipe.

'You been trying to get Miss Gretchen to say I was up at the house on Saturday,' began Fisher challengingly.

Gently removed his pipe. 'Well – weren't you?' he asked.

'That's what you'd like to know, isn't it? That's what you've been getting at all the while?'

'It's one of the things,' admitted Gently.

'And now you're going to hear about it – straight – just like it happened!'

Gently blew an opulent smoke-ring. 'You wouldn't like to step into headquarters for this little scene, I suppose?' he enquired.

'What – and have it all taken down and twisted about by you blokes? What a hope!' Fisher laughed raucously. 'You just listen to it here, if you want to listen.'

Gently nodded gravely. 'There's just one thing I'd like to know first . . . why are you telling me this now, when you took such pains to hide it before?'

Fisher glowered at him. 'It's on account of you getting at Miss Gretchen.'

'I didn't think you worried a great deal about Miss Gretchen these days.'

'I aren't worried about her – but if she's going to tell her tale then I'm going to tell mine . . . see?'

'Sort of getting it in first . . .' murmured Gently.

'Never you mind.' Fisher came a little closer to Gently, but getting into the line of fire of the smoke-rings he moved back again. 'Listen,' he said, 'just suppose I was there that afternoon – suppose he was there – suppose we were in her room together all the time that was going on – that don't make us murderers, does it?'

'It makes you liars,' said Gently affably.

'But it don't make us murderers . . . that's the thing. Naturally, you weren't going to expect us to be mixed up in it if we could help it.'

'Not even with a man's life at stake?'

'Well, how could us being mixed up in it help him?'

'You're telling me,' said Gently. 'Just keep right on.'

'All right, then, so I was there. I got in through the kitchen while there wasn't no one there and went up into her room.'

'What time was that?'

'How the hell should I know what time it was? It was after lunch, that's all I know about it. She come up a little bit later on.'

'With a cup of coffee?'

'All right – she'd got a cup of coffee! And I suppose you'd like to know what we was doing up there, as well?'

'No,' said Gently, 'no, it might amuse the jury, but it isn't strictly relevant . . . pass on to the next bit.'

'Well, then, during the afternoon there was somebody come to the door, and I go out on the landing to see who it is . . . like you know, it was Mr Peter. Miss Gretchen, she come out too. We stood there listening to what was going on . . . you could hear some of it up on the landing. Then the old man shrieked, and Miss Gretchen she go rushing down to see what had happened.'

'Why didn't you go?' asked Gently.

'I wasn't bloody well supposed to be there, was I? We didn't know the old boy was done for . . . anyway, back she come and tell me what it is, so I say: "You and me is outside this – we'll go out and make it look like we haven't been here this afternoon," and that's what we did, Mr Inspector Gently, so now you know.'

Gently puffed three rings, one inside the other. 'You went out through the study,' he said, 'so you saw the body. Where was it lying?'

'It was by the safe. You don't think we moved it, do you?'

'How was it lying?'

'It was face down with the legs shoved up a bit.'

'Was the knife there?'

'. . . I can't remember every squitting little thing!'

'But this isn't a squitting little thing, and it's not one you're likely to have missed. Was it there?'

'I tell you I can't remember . . .!'

'Was it because you didn't look very closely . . . because it wasn't, in fact, the first time you had seen the body?'

Fisher's eyes blazed at him. 'All bloody right! It was there – stuck in up to the hilt. Now are you satisfied?'

Gently smiled up towards Burgh Street. 'I'm beginning to be . . .' he said.

'You're still trying to get me to say I see it done – that's what you're at!'

Gently shrugged and puffed smoke.

'You may try – but it isn't going to get you anywhere, see? I've told you what happened that afternoon, just like it was, and I'll swear to it in court if need be. But that's all you're getting out of me!'

'Even if Peter Huysmann hangs?'

'If he got into trouble that's his look-out – not mine.'

Gently sighed, and turned to regard a blue-chalk mannequin which leered surrealistically from an obstinate patch of plaster. He poked it tentatively. It came crashing down amongst the nettles. 'That girl Susan . . . she certainly gets around,' he said.

'What do you mean by that?' growled Fisher.

'Oh . . . it was just a passing thought. Aren't you taking her out tonight?'

'Suppose I am – what's it got to do with you?'

'It just set me wondering . . . that's all.'

Fisher towered above the Chief Inspector in stupid rage. 'And so you may bloody well wonder!' he burst out, 'you and all the other coppers with you . . . if I want to take her out, I take her out . . . and you can wonder till the bloody sky drops on you!'

Gently clicked his tongue disappointedly. 'I thought you were going to say till a bit of wall dropped on me,' he said.

CHAPTER TWELVE

MRS TURNER ANSWERED the door when Gently knocked at the Huysmann house. She eyed him inimically with her small mean eyes – she had had her knife into him since the questioning. 'So *you're* here again,' she said. Gently admitted it gracefully. 'A fine one you are, coming and upsetting people with your silly questions – don't even belong here, either. What do you want this time?'

'I want to see Miss Gretchen again.'

'Oh, you do? Well, I'm afraid you're going to be disappointed. Miss Gretchen's gone out.'

'Where's she gone?'

'How should I know where she's gone?'

'It's rather important that I should see her just now.'

Mrs Turner snorted and tilted her chin. 'Strikes me it's always important when *you* want to see somebody – leastways, that's your idea. And it's on account of you she's gone out . . . upsetting her like that!'

'Have you any idea where she might be?'

'I told you I hadn't . . . might be the Castle, or Earton Park . . . she used to go there sometimes.'

'Thank you,' said Gently, and the door was promptly slammed. Shaking his head, he plodded off towards the city. The Castle . . . or Earton Park. Or anywhere else in a city of rising a hundred and fifty thou. He took the Castle first because it lay in his way. Stretching halfway round the base of the Castle's prehistoric mound was the Garden, where once had been the ditch, a crescenting walk, deep-sunken, bisected by the slanting stone bridge which connected the Castle with the cattle market. Here were people enough, strolling amongst the long, sweet-scented beds of wallflowers and beneath the carnival blossom of the Japanese cherry-trees. But there was no Gretchen. Gently glanced up through the elms at the sleepy-faced Castle . . . but one didn't seek consolation amongst stuffed birds and man-traps. He went out to the Paddock and sought a bus for Earton Park.

It was a nice park, but a very large one. Its extent and complexity brought a pout to Gently's lips. But having come, he set about the matter methodically and plodded away across the rose parterre to the avenue of chestnuts, on either side of which old gentlemen were playing interminable games of bowls. Beyond these were the tennis-courts, on which Gently wasted no more than a passing glance. Coming to the Circus with its cupola'd bandstand he paused in indecision. North? South? Long, frequented vistas stretched to the four cardinal points. He took a chief inspectorial sniff and went south.

It was a good sniff. He found Gretchen huddled on a seat beside the great lily pond, staring large-eyed at the shallow water. Gently lifted his brown trilby politely and seated himself at a suitable distance.

Gretchen said: 'I did not know that you would find me here.'

'I didn't know myself until I found you,' Gently replied, feeling about for his pipe.

'Please do not think that I came here specially to avoid you . . . it was just that I had to get away . . . I could not think in the house.'

'I think you were wise . . . a change of venue is helpful.'

Gently went slowly and carefully through the business of filling and lighting his pipe, tamped it down with his thumb and took one or two inaugurating puffs. 'Have you come to any decision?' he asked.

Gretchen turned towards him pitifully. 'It is very difficult . . . I do not know.'

'Perhaps I can help you. I've just been having a very interesting chat with our friend Fisher.'

'. . . Fisher?'

'Yes.'

'And he has said something?'

Gently nodded.

She studied him for a moment in silence, Gently puffing away unconcernedly. 'I do not know . . .' she said.

'You'll have to take my word for it, of course. He admitted that he spent the afternoon with you, that he was there when you discovered the murder, and that it was at his suggestion that you went out and got yourself alibis. Is that correct?'

'He said all . . . that?' Gretchen stared at him incredulously.

'That was the gist of it, though I'm not quite satisfied.'

She looked away from him, her hands beginning to clutch together. 'I cannot understand . . . why should he tell you that?'

'Oh, there's no mystery about why he told me. He's rather thick with Susan these days and she told him how I'd been questioning you this morning . . . I gather she was listening at the door. This seems to have worried Mr Fisher and he hastened to put his story on record.'

'. . . Susan?'

'She seems to be Fisher's latest acquisition.'

'It is not true – you must not speak about him like that!'

Gently shrugged. 'I think you foster a somewhat idealistic opinion of Fisher, Miss Gretchen . . . however, that's why he told his story. Perhaps he will verify it if you ask him.'

'No!' She shook her head vigorously. 'I do not want to speak to him . . . not ever again. Later, I will get a new chauffeur.'

Gently regarded his pipe-smoke rising tenuously in the still, warm air. 'Were you ever really in love with him, Miss Gretchen?' he asked.

Gretchen turned her head away. 'I think that I was, once upon a time.'

'You knew what sort of character he had – I mean, with women?'

'Oh yes . . . I must have known that. It is as you say, I had an idealistic opinion. In my situation such things happen easily . . . we can believe when we want to.'

'And yet now, when the way is clear, you have turned completely against him.'

Gretchen hung her head and said nothing.

'Did you ever think of marrying him?' Gently asked.

176

'Oh yes, I used to think of that. I thought perhaps, when my father died . . . but that is a very terrible thing to say.'

'And did Fisher know that?'

'We used to talk about it.'

'He knew, then, that once your father was out of the way he could expect to be your husband?'

Gretchen wrenched her hands viciously, one from the other. 'But we did not think of this – we did not think of this!'

'Are you quite certain in your own mind that Fisher did not think of this?'

'No – no! he did not!' A shudder ran through her body, and she crouched away from Gently, over the arm of the seat.

'Miss Gretchen, I am asking you again: why is it that you have now turned against Fisher?'

'I don't know . . . I don't believe in him any longer.'

'Then what has shaken your faith in him so suddenly . . . precisely at this juncture?'

Gretchen moaned but made no answer.

'Let me ask you another question. Whose finger-prints did you suppose you wiped from the handle of the knife – your brother's, or Fisher's?'

'I have told you . . . my brother's!'

Gently leaned away, shaking his head. 'Miss Gretchen, I have still to learn the truth of your and Fisher's actions on Saturday afternoon.'

There was a long pause, broken by nothing but the distant calls from the tennis-courts and the dull murmur of traffic from behind trees. Above the low hedge at the bottom moved a white triangle. It was the sail of a model yacht on the second pond, further down. The triangle shuddered, stopped, wagged a moment, then slowly sank from sight as the model slid away on its new course. Gently watched the little performance impassively. 'They've opened the refreshment bar . . .' he said. 'Let's go and have a cup of tea.'

He sat Gretchen down at one of the little tile-topped tables by a french window and fetched tea from the counter in large, thick cups. Gretchen stirred her tea at some length. Just outside a foursome was being played, a young and a middle-aged couple: other tennis-players sat in groups round the larger tables, chattering and drinking soft drinks from bottles.

Gently sipped his tea and then leaned forward, chin in hand. Gretchen gave him a frightened glance. He said: 'It will have to be told some time . . . why not tell me now?'

'But . . . how can I?'

'Is it so damning, what you know?'

'To you it may seem so . . .'

Gently felt down for his tea-cup. 'At least, you ought to warn Susan what sort of person she's taking on.'

'Susan!' The waxen cheeks flushed.

'She's going out with him tonight.'

'What do I care about that?'

'Well, having done it once and got away with it . . .' He took another sip of tea and appeared to be watching the foursome through the french window. Gretchen laid a trembling teaspoon in her saucer.

'He told you so much . . . of his own accord?'

Gently shrugged imperceptibly. 'Nobody forced him . . . he buttonholed me in the street.'

'It was because he thinks I have spoken . . .?'

Gently said nothing, continued to watch the foursome fumble its way through another service. There was a burst of laughter from the party at the higher table: 'Harry wouldn't do a thing like that . . . no, no, we can't believe it!' 'But he did, I tell you!' 'Johnny, you're only saying that because Vera's here . . .' They clattered their bottles together and trooped out.

'How about it?' mused Gently.

'Must it be . . . now?'

'It will help me, and you'll feel better to have done with it.'

'Yes . . . I shall feel better.' She gave a deep sigh and faced him. 'Very well . . . it is as you say. I wiped the prints off the knife because I think he did it.'

'And why did you think that?'

'He was not with me then . . . at the time my father was killed.'

'Where was he?'

She shook her head. 'He went down as soon as my brother had gone to the study.'

'Where – into the passage?'

'That is so, but I remained on the landing. I heard the quarrel. After it is over, I expect him to come back up, but he did not come . . . and then there is the scream.'

'About how long would it be between the time the quarrel ended and the time you heard the scream?'

'Two, three minutes.'

'And you went down immediately on hearing the scream?'

'Oh no! It was frightening to hear that . . . I did not dare to go down then. It was another minute or two before I had courage to go. Then it was as I told you . . . I found him near the safe.'

'And you saw nobody?'

'Nobody . . . except my father.'

'About how long were you in the room?'

'It seemed a long time, but it was just a little while.'

'And during that time you heard nothing?'

'I should not have heard . . . once, everything went black and I thought I would fall. Then I came to myself again, and I knew I must do something . . . something to stop people thinking that it was him.'

'You had no doubt in your mind then that Fisher was the murderer?'

'. . . no, I had no doubt.'

'Have you had any doubt since that time?'

'. . . no.'

'Where did you next see him?'

'He was waiting in the bedroom when I got back. He asked me where I had been . . . when I told him that my father was killed he pretended to be surprised.'

'And it was he who suggested establishing alibis?'

'Oh yes . . . he said that I might have gone out through the kitchen, just as he had come in . . . there was nothing to prove that we had ever been there. He told me to find out about the programme at a cinema and it would be all right.'

'And you left by the study and the timber-yard?'

'That is so.'

'As you were passing through the study, did Fisher stop to examine the body?'

'No . . . he went straight through . . . I do not think he looked at it.'

Gently brooded over his cooling tea. 'All this . . .' he said, 'you know, it's your word against Fisher's.'

'But it is the truth!'

Gently smiled at a part-submerged tea-leaf. 'I believe you . . . what you tell me fits every fact it touches. But I wish there was some proof, just a little bit. Because without it, one could even make a case against you, Miss Gretchen . . . and it wouldn't be a bad one at that.'

There was a tea-time air about headquarters – against the run of the play, because nothing at headquarters was ever quite normal; but the human touch had its occasional triumphs, and this was one. Gently sniffed as he passed the canteen. They were serving toast and its cosy, inviting smell warned him that even the best of lunches wears off by five o'clock. The toast smell carried over to the superintendent's office, where the great man was sitting ingesting a plateful, a far-away look in his eyes. The look became present and immediate when Gently entered.

'I was just thinking about you,' he said.

Gently acknowledged the thought with the ghost of a bow, moved over and abstracted half a round of toast from the super's plate. 'Of course, if you're hungry . . .' observed the super bitterly. Gently disclaimed the imputation through his first mouthful.

The super said: 'Well?'

'I'm almost home,' returned Gently, butteredly.

'You've got a case made out?'

'It's made out, but it won't stand up yet. All the same, I think I've got enough to let young Peter out . . . so it's a good thing you held back on him.'

The super ate some toast nastily. 'Give,' he said.

Gently crunched a moment. 'First, I've had a statement from Fisher to the effect that he was in the house that afternoon.'

The super's eyes opened wide. 'You mean he's talked?' he fired.

'He's talked, but he hasn't talked enough – not yet. That's the main problem ahead, and I think it's going to be solved without a great deal of difficulty.'

'What do you mean by that?'

'I mean I've persuaded Miss Gretchen to fill in some of the gaps. According to her testimony, Fisher must either have seen it done or done it himself, one or the other. Of course, it's her word against Fisher's, but Fisher is getting to be rather worried, and if you make a pass at him with a murder charge I fancy he'll talk both loud and clear.'

The super brandished a piece of toast. 'Wait a minute!' he exclaimed. 'Do I understand that both of them were in the house at the time of the murder? They've both admitted that?'

Gently nodded pontifically. 'Fisher made a voluntary statement. I had to spend some time on Miss Gretchen. At first she insisted that she was there alone, but after I got Fisher's statement she came across with it. She has been positive that Fisher did it from the first – it was she who wiped the knife and hid it. She's in trouble, by the way. Fisher became her lover a month or two ago and Saturday afternoon was his regular visiting time.'

'Give me time!' pleaded the super. 'I'm still holding Peter Huysmann – doesn't he fit into this thing anywhere?'

'Well, he was there, and his quarrel with his father may have suggested to the murderer that the time was ripe.

Otherwise, I don't think he has much to do with the business.'

'You're saying that Fisher got the girl into trouble and then bumped off the old man so that he could marry her . . . is that it?'

'Could be,' admitted Gently cautiously, 'but there's another angle to it . . .'

'Never mind the other angle! Let's get this one straightened out first. You say the girl was sure that Fisher did it?'

Gently finished his piece of toast and licked his fingers. 'Fisher came in through the kitchen just after lunch and went upstairs to Gretchen's room. There was nobody in the kitchen and nobody saw him enter. Gretchen went up with her coffee and stayed there with him. When Peter arrived they went out on the landing to see who it was – Fisher was the person Peter caught sight of – and directly he had gone to the study Fisher left Gretchen on the landing and went into the passage. Gretchen heard the quarrel from the landing. It ended, and she waited two or three minutes for Fisher to come back, but he didn't come back, and at the end of that two or three minutes she heard the old man's death scream.

'By the time she pulled herself together and went down the murderer had gone. She met nobody in the passage and saw nobody in the study, and feeling certain that Fisher was the man, she took away the knife and wiped the prints off the handle. When she got back to the bedroom Fisher was already there. He expressed surprise when she told him what she had found, and suggested going out and establishing the alibis. They went out by the study and the timber-yard. Fisher exhibited no interest in the body when he passed it. I discovered by questioning that he was not even aware that the knife had been removed. Fisher's version differs inasmuch as he claims that he never left the landing, otherwise they pretty well agree.'

'Then he *was* the person in the drawing-room?' interrupted the super, biting mechanically at a fresh piece of toast.

'Unquestionably. Otherwise, he could not have got back to the bedroom without being seen by Gretchen. Of course, we don't know at what point he entered. He may have gone in straight away, watched the quarrel, seen the murder, seen Gretchen go in and then slipped back to the bedroom . . . or he may not.'

'You're telling me he may not! But what about the money?'

'I'm not sure about that. If Fisher was the murderer I think he must have come back for it, after he'd got rid of Gretchen. He might have come back for it anyway, though I don't think it's likely. At all events there was too much of it to carry about his person. There is, incidentally, some indication that Fisher has come into money just recently.'

'And that's one of the seven deadly sins in criminal investigation.' The super's eyes glistened. 'By God, Gently, you certainly get results. I'll let this be a lesson to me.'

Gently shook his head. 'It's mostly one witness against another at the moment. We've got to have proof.'

'We'll get proof. I'll get a warrant and take his flat apart, brick by brick, and if the money's there we'll find it. And I'll make him talk, if I have to question him from now to Christmas.'

'He won't talk if he's the murderer.'

'Then if he doesn't talk I'll charge him with it.'

'I shouldn't be too hasty about that . . .' began Gently, and broke off. Hansom came striding into the room, followed by Police Constable Letts. 'Look at this!' boomed Hansom, 'look at this!' And he waved a limp piece of paper under the super's nose. The super stared at it. 'What is it?' he asked. 'What is it!' 'It's another of the Huysmann notes – it's just been turned in by the bank!'

The super grabbed it as though it were a rare visitant from another world. 'Where did they get it?' he exclaimed.

'It was paid in this afternoon by "The Doll's Hospital".'

'By the *what*?'

' "The Doll's Hospital".'

The super goggled at Hansom. 'And what the blazing blue hell is "The Doll's Hospital" . . .?'

'Excuse me, sir . . .' Constable Letts slid round the mass that was Hansom. '"The Doll's Hospital" is a toy-shop in St Benedict's, sir.'

'And what the devil has that got to do with the Huysmann case?'

Gently said: 'What sort of toy-shop is it?'

'It's one of those that goes in for Meccano sets and that sort of thing, sir.'

'Does it sell scale model aeroplanes?'

'Yes, sir. It's got a window full of them.'

'Fisher!' yipped Hansom, catching on with commendable suddenness. 'He told us he built scale models in his spare time.'

The super shot a meaningful glance at Gently. 'You wanted proof, by golly . . .!' He turned to Hansom.

'We're pulling in Fisher right away. Wait here till I get warrants – I'm in on this party – and send a patrol car round to his flat.'

Ten minutes later the super's Humber bumbled over the ruts of Paradise Alley and pulled up beside the patrol car. A police sergeant ran round and saluted. 'There doesn't seem to be anybody at home, sir,' he said.

'Is the door locked?' snapped the super.

'Yes, sir.'

'Smash it in, then.'

'Very good, sir.'

The super, Gently and Hansom climbed out and watched the sergeant direct smashing operations. It was not the best of doors. It yielded easily to one constable-power. The super, eager to draw blood, went bounding up the narrow stairs, Hansom in close pursuit. Gently followed at a more sedate pace. 'He's not here!' bawled Hansom, emerging from the bedroom. 'Try the lounge,' suggested Gently, 'it's a bit before his bedtime . . .' He wandered into the kitchen after the super, who was making great play with a wall-cupboard full of junk. 'Hell's . . . *bells!*' came from Hansom. 'Chiefy – for God's sake come and look at this lot!' 'What have you found, Hansom?' barked the super. 'Just come and look at it!' The super bounced across the dingy landing, Gently following. Hansom stood back, tallow-faced.

Sprawled on the floor of the sitting-room, mouth open, eyes staring, was Fisher. His throat was cut down from the ear on the right side. A blood-stained razor, which Gently recognized, lay near his right hand and on the couch near him, neatly stacked, stood a fabulous pile of treasury notes.

CHAPTER THIRTEEN

G ENTLY, HAVING SEEN enough, went out and sat in the Humber while the police medico made his examination. After him came the photographer, whose flash-bulbs could be seen popping through the unmasked window. Hansom and the super came out in conference with the medico. '. . . Naturally, it's always possible,' said the medico, 'any self-inflicted wound *may* have been the result of an attack . . . we can only offer proof the other way round, viz., that a certain wound could *not* have been self-inflicted. But there is no suggestion of that here. I am perfectly satisfied that this is a bona fide case of suicide.'

'I wasn't querying the present case,' grunted the super. 'I could see that for myself with half an eye.'

Hansom said: 'And Gently recognizes the razor . . . it's the one he cut out the models with.'

They came up to the car and Gently got out. 'You might well say that Fisher was getting worried,' said the super to him, a trifle grimly.

'He didn't seem so terribly worried when I last saw him . . . just a bit on edge.'

The super shook his head. 'You must put the fear of the Lord into people without realizing it. Well ... I suppose it's saved a deal of trouble and expense, though personally I should have got a lot of satisfaction out of putting him in dock. We can let young Huysmann go now.'

Hansom said: 'I still can't quite get this straight ... I feel like a kid who's got his sums wrong. But I hand it to you, Gently. You were right and I was wrong ... I reckon they don't put you in the Central Office at the Yard for nothing.'

'You weren't the only one who was wrong,' growled the super. 'It just goes to show ... you need specialists when it comes to homicide.' He glanced at Gently, half-admiring, half-jealous. 'I suppose it gets to be an instinct when someone's been on the job as long as you have.'

Gently shrugged. 'I started with an advantage ... I saw young Huysmann riding on the Wall. One doesn't do that sort of thing straight after murdering one's father.'

'All the same ... it was a top-grade job.'

Gently smiled wanly at them. 'I'm glad you're pleased with me, just this once,' he said, 'because you're not going to be pleased with me for very long.'

'What? How do you mean, Gently?' The super glanced at him quickly.

'I mean that unlike yourselves, I do *not* regard the death of Fisher as being suicide.'

'*What!*'

'On the contrary, I am as positive as my specialization and acquired instinct can make me that it's murder.'

There was a pause, fraught and ominous. Three pairs

of eyes stared at Gently as though he had suddenly touched their owners with three red-hot pokers.

'You're off your chump!' bawled Hansom, finding his voice. 'You – you've got murder on the brain!'

'It's utterly preposterous!' snapped the police doctor.

'Really, Gently, I completely fail to understand—!'

Gently bowed and let the storm pass over his head. 'I don't expect you to agree with me until you've heard my reasons . . . but that is my conviction.'

'But there is nothing – nothing whatever to suggest an attack!'

'It's the stupidest thing I ever heard!'

Gently turned to the furious little police doctor. 'Were you able to form an opinion as to the direction in which the cut was made?' he enquired mildly.

'Direction? What in the world has that got to do with it?'

'I'd like to have your opinion.'

'As far as I can say it was made upwards, from the base of the throat to the ear. But—!'

'If the cut were self-inflicted, isn't it more likely to have been made in the other direction . . . from the ear downwards?'

The little man fumed at him. 'It could be made in either direction – it is only slightly more likely to have been made downwards.'

'And wouldn't you say it was still more likely to have been made on the left side of the throat . . . bearing in mind that the razor was ostensibly held in his right hand?'

'I think this is all highly irrelevant, Gently!' broke in the super. 'It's ridiculous to suppose that you can deduce murder from such trivial considerations.'

'I'm not deducing murder from them . . . I'm simply demonstrating that the cut was made in the least likely of three ways.'

'But there is no guarantee that a suicide will choose the likeliest way! If you had seen as many suicides as I have . . .!' The medico, his professional skill called to question, fairly chattered with rage. 'And how likely would it be for an attacker to make the cut upwards? You tell me that! How do you attack a man and cut his throat in that direction?'

Gently extended a disclaiming palm. 'Suppose you had to cut Fisher's throat . . . how would you do it?'

'It is not a question of how I would do it!'

'But suppose you did?'

The little man glared at him. 'I should do it – like this!' And he made a downward slash that whistled past Gently's neck.

Gently shook his head gravely. 'You'd be a very brave man to do that,' he said, 'much braver than I should be . . . also, you'd have to be lucky. Now if I wanted to cut Fisher's throat . . . neatly, and without noise and personal danger . . . I should wait till he was bending over something . . . something like a bag containing forty thousand pounds, and then I'd do it – like this!' And he spun the little doctor round, pushed him into a bending position, and drew his right hand smartly across his struggling victim's throat.

'I should also be in a good position to avoid the subsequent rush of blood,' he added, thoughtfully.

'All right, Gently, you've shown us that it could be done!' snapped the super, 'and where precisely do we go from there?'

'That's right,' echoed Hansom, 'who's it going to be this time – the housekeeper?'

Gently said: 'The person who killed Fisher was the same person whom Fisher saw killing Huysmann. He killed Fisher for three reasons. First, Fisher was blackmailing him. Second, there was a risk that the money he paid Fisher would be traced back to Fisher, and thus to himself. Third, he knew that I had discovered his motive for killing Huysmann, and that he would have to make some sort of move to draw the police off. Unfortunately, I didn't realize he would make it quite so soon.'

'And who is this mythical person, Gently?'

'He is Leaming, Huysmann's manager.'

Hansom set up a howl. 'What – Leaming kill the old man? You're bats – completely bats! Why, Leaming had the one alibi that stood the steam-test – he's fire-proof!'

'It was a good alibi,' Gently admitted reluctantly, 'but that's all it was – an alibi. He probably parked his car at the ground, where no doubt it was known to the attendants. There was then nothing to prevent him from making his way through the crowd back to the yard. I am not certain of his exact movements, but I imagine that he watched the quarrel from the summer-house and emerged from it soon after Peter Huysmann left. With regard to the alibi, I questioned him about the football match on the Saturday evening before he had time to gen up on it. He had three things to tell me about it and they formed the three headlines in the pink'un, in exactly the same sequence. On the following day he had the match at his fingertips – he even knew the precise minutes when the scores were made, a detail which a man on the terrace is never aware of.

'Also on Saturday evening – and later during the questioning – he introduced obliquely every point which would tell against Peter. Under cover of a pretended solicitude he suggested things which were absolutely damning – such things as Huysmann's resolution to cut Peter out of his will, which he represented as being of recent origin. In addition to this . . .'

'Hold hard!' broke in the super, 'you're making my head spin, Gently. There doesn't seem to be any end to you. When you made your report in the office an hour ago it was Fisher, Fisher, Fisher. So we go out, and find it was Fisher. And immediately you turn the record over and begin on Leaming. If this isn't a sudden spasm of madness, would you mind telling me why you didn't mention Leaming in the office, but only now when the case has cancelled itself out?'

Gently sighed deeply, and felt around for the support of a peppermint cream. 'I was going to tell you about Leaming,' he said, 'but I didn't get a chance. You're all so impulsive round here. I'd just got through telling you what I knew about Fisher when Hansom came in with the note and you straightway jumped to the conclusion that Fisher was the man. *I* didn't say he was . . . in fact, I was pretty certain that he wasn't, and what we've found up there convinces me to the hilt. Fisher was an extrovert if ever there was one – he would no more have cut his throat than spoken English. But you got so sold on the idea, and I wanted Fisher picked up for questioning . . . so I let the rest of it ride till we'd laid hands on him.'

'Then you're not just hanging out this case for the fun of it?'

Gently looked shocked. 'Really, superintendent!'

'All right, all right! Now – you say Leaming killed Huysmann. Why?'

'Because Huysmann had discovered how Leaming bought his cars and his houses and his hand-made cigarettes.'

'And how did he do that?'

'He was flogging timber on the side, about one-fifth of the entire intake . . . twelve thousand pounds' worth a year. That was the leak which Peter said his father suspected, and it had been going on quite a few years. Mind you, Leaming didn't scoop the entire twelve thousand. The tug-skipper and his mate were in it, though I don't think they knew much, and there was a mysterious firm called "The Straight Grain Timber Merchants" who took the stuff away. I imagine they're dissolved as from today, but we might get a line on them . . . the tug-men may talk, with a little persuasion. There's another angle in the books. I went through the Huysmann books on Sunday, so I knew the "Straight Grain" outfit was not in the regular line of business with them. Leaming has got a very thin excuse that they kept separate books for the "Straight Grain" transactions and he's prepared to produce them: I think an expert comparison between the two sets of books will give us an opening.'

The super said: 'Granted that you're right about Leaming's fiddling, how do you know that Huysmann had found out about it?'

Gently drew out his wallet and produced the green postcard. 'I found this in Huysmann's desk. According to Miss Gretchen it is the most recently received card – it is postmarked on the twentieth – and Huysmann took it with the rest of his mail on his last trip to London.

Ostensibly it was during this trip that he got scent of the "Straight Grain" set-up, and though he may not have tumbled to the significance of it straight away, his suspicions were aroused and he made this note of the name. That gives us a further angle. If we trace Huysmann's movements on that trip we may find the source of his information . . . though the trail has got a little sketchy now Fisher's dead.

'When he got back off his trip I imagine Huysmann began to make some guarded enquiries about "Straight Grain". He apparently found out enough, and it's my conjecture that his visit to Leaming's office last thing on Saturday morning was to summon Leaming to produce an immediate explanation. It isn't difficult to imagine Leaming's reaction to that. He might be able to satisfy other people with his twin set of books, but there was no prospect of satisfying Huysmann. He faced a long term of imprisonment, plus utter ruination – you will remember in conjunction with this that the last firm he managed went bankrupt, though he got clear from that one – and Leaming was not the sort of man to let that happen if there was a loop-hole. And there was a loop-hole. He could silence Huysmann.

'Consider for a moment how favourable the circumstances were for such a step. First, it was well known that Leaming spent his Saturday afternoons at the football. Second, it was known that he proposed to spend that Saturday afternoon at the football – he would have warned his housekeeper that he wanted lunch promptly, and his gardener was expecting to get a lift down with him. Third, nobody knew that Huysmann had summoned him to his study. Fourth, the study was isolated from the rest of the house, and fifth, it could be entered quite secretly by way of the yard.

'Everything, then, favoured the attempt. I don't know whether the theft of the money was premeditated, because he didn't know that the safe was going to be open. It may have been an afterthought when he saw Peter given one of the notes, or to suggest an outside job if Peter got off, or simply from greed. With regard to weapons, you will notice that in both murders he used the weapon on the spot, that they were the same class of weapon, and that they were used from the same position – behind. The knives in the study he had always known about. You will remember how well they were placed for an attacker entering from the garden – especially a tall attacker. The razor he had undoubtedly seen on his previous visit to the flat . . . I am conjecturing that he went to the flat previously for his first deal with Fisher.

'Huysmann, then, was disposed of, with the unlooked-for piece of luck of Peter being on the spot to collect the blame. Leaming's alibi was fire-proof, he made a good impression on the police, and a little annoyance of myself asking to see the books could be attributed to a policeman's officiousness. Everything was going swimmingly . . . until Monday morning. On Monday morning Fisher visited Leaming's office – I saw him – and Leaming made the spine-chilling discovery that the murder had been witnessed. And it had not been witnessed by his best friend.

'The bone of contention between Leaming and Fisher was the maid, Susan. Fisher had always had a fancy for her, but he was never in the running – it took money to get Susan – and he bore Leaming a deep grudge about her. Naturally, with Leaming completely in his power, his first demand was for Susan . . . with a small cut in the forty thou, to be going on with. And he got her. That same evening Leaming picked her up and brought her into town, told her abruptly that everything was over and left her flat. The deal then was for Fisher to take up the running, but he was a little late on cue. Susan, reacting to a crisis like most women, went in search of a cup of tea, and while she was getting it she bumped into me. She told me the story without much prompting – also, she told me about Fisher's affair with Gretchen and about Gretchen's pregnancy. I kept her by me the rest of the evening . . . when we left the café Fisher was there, watching. Later in the evening I met him at Charlie's, in Queen Street, and he tried to find out what Susan had told me.

'Fisher was beginning to get worried by then. I had been up to his flat in the morning and he had seen me interrogating a little boy who makes a playground of the ruins up there, and probably guessed – which was a fact – that I had obtained an account of his movements on Saturday afternoon which did not tally with the one he'd put on record. Also, I hinted to him that I knew of his affair with Gretchen. This upset him so much that he made his clumsy attempt at inspectorcide . . . I was beginning to know far too much.'

'Then it was Fisher who tried to drop the masonry on you?' broke in the super. 'Why didn't you tell me that yesterday?'

Gently's shoulders rose a fraction. 'There wasn't any proof . . . it just happened that the masonry was dropped on me immediately after I had interviewed him, from a vantage point familiar to him and which he could have attained in the interval.

'With Fisher worried but nowhere near cracking, I decided that Gretchen was my best move, so this morning I interviewed her and got part of her story. I might have got the rest of it then and there, but oddly enough, just as she was working up to it, we were interrupted by Leaming, who hung around with a blanket of small talk until Gretchen cooled off and wouldn't come across. You can imagine that if Fisher was worried, Leaming had got the feeling that he was living on the edge of a volcano, and one that was beginning to rumble ominously. Quite apart from the notes turning up, Fisher was behaving in a way that drew attention to himself – boasting of the changes that were going to take place, and the things he could tell the police if he wanted to – and there was no telling when he would start throwing the money about, thus raising immediate suspicion. In addition to this something had gone wrong about Peter – he hadn't been charged. And there was myself, working on Gretchen, and Gretchen just about to spill the beans.

'All in all, things seemed to be going to pieces in an alarming manner and he invited me to lunch to get from me, if he could, the precise state of affairs. He certainly got value for money. I showed him the card, which I had just found, and showed a good deal of scepticism for his explanation of the "Straight Grain" business . . . especially when he admitted himself unable to produce their address. He knew then that I'd seen past Fisher, that I understood his motive. It only remained for me to crack Fisher – and I could do that fairly easily by getting Gretchen to talk – actually, it became easier still, because Fisher made a partial statement which was instrumental in making Gretchen talk.

'Thus it was merely a question of time and routine before Leaming stood revealed . . . and not very much of either. Somehow he had to break the chain that was forging round him and break it in such a way that it would never come together again. And there was only one way to do that – to get rid of Fisher. With Fisher gone, all direct evidence was swept away . . . and if it could be made to look like suicide, with the money carefully planted, then the trail would come to a dead end. Suspicion of embezzlement might remain, but that would be all.

'I don't know whether he had an arrangement to deliver the rest of the money to Fisher this afternoon, but that is what happened, and the murder took place as I described it . . . I am certain of that because there is some blood on the notes, which there would not have been unless they were closer to Fisher when his throat was cut than when we found them. The evidence to look for in that connection will be the bag in which the notes were brought, which is bound to have extensive blood-stains. We can print the notes, of course, but my feeling is that Leaming is too careful a man not to have used gloves.'

Gently broke off, glancing at the three silent men in the lengthening twilight. 'Well . . . that's my case,' he said, 'it hasn't become any easier with the loss of Fisher, but as far as I'm concerned, it's become absolutely positive.'

The super took a long breath and bored into Gently with his sharp, authoritative eyes. 'So that's your case, is it?' he enquired icily.

Gently nodded without expression. There was a moment or two's silence, emphasized by the distant rumble of traffic, below them in Queen Street and above them in Burgh Street.

Hansom said: 'It stinks, if you ask me.'

'It's childish!' snapped the little doctor. 'I stake my reputation on suicide.'

'You could put that alibi through a rolling mill.'

The super frowned, still boring at Gently. 'You realize that I have a very high opinion of you . . . especially after what you've achieved so far,' he said, 'and I admit that I am to a certain extent impressed with what you have been telling us. I believe that you believe it, and I believe that you've got something about Leaming and the "Straight Grain" business. But really, Gently, have you got anything else? I mean, look at it from my point of view. Three parts of this case of yours is conjecture and for the rest you offer no vital proof. It's ingenious and not improbable, but what else can you say for it?'

Gently said, woodenly: 'We can get the proofs . . . if we work at it.'

'But proofs of what? If we follow up the lines you indicate we may be able to show that Leaming was a large-scale embezzler and we may be able to show that Huysmann found out about it, but how does that make Leaming the murderer? You say yourself that with Fisher gone, the trail has come to a dead end. If there is anything in what you suspect, Fisher's evidence was the lynch-pin, and we've lost it. What else is there that a counsel wouldn't shoot to fragments? You say that Fisher was blackmailing Leaming. Where's the proof? You say that Fisher got the maid off him – but isn't it just as likely that Leaming broke with her because he had ideas about Gretchen? You say that Leaming's information about the football match was derived from the pink'un . . . well, how are you going to make that stand up?'

'I haven't done with that one yet . . .'

'You've got thirty thousand interrogations ahead of you!' jeered Hansom.

The super cocked his head on one side. 'It's no good, Gently, you haven't got a case, not even the makings of one. If it's as you say, it can never be proved. And in the meanwhile, there's nothing in Fisher's behaviour in conflict with the view that he was the murderer and the thief.'

'Except that he wasn't the suicide type.'

'There isn't any suicide type!' broke in the little doctor. 'Anybody will commit suicide under certain conditions.'

'Fisher would have stood trial . . . he was too stupid to want to have avoided it.'

'That's quite ridiculous!'

The super said: 'Even there you've only shown that murder was possible, and it's possible in the majority of suicide cases. You cannot show that murder was likely.'

Gently brooded, felt for another peppermint cream. 'You've searched the flat?' he asked absently.

'Of course we've searched the flat.'

'You've been through his pockets?'

'Naturally.'

'And you found the key?'

The super stared at Gently uncomprehendingly. 'What key?'

'The door-key of the flat . . . it wasn't in the door.'

'What are you getting at, Gently?'

Gently ate the peppermint cream slowly and irritatingly. 'The door was locked,' he mumbled, 'if Fisher locked it, you should be able to find the key.'

Hansom said: 'He'd got a key-ring in his pocket.'

'One doesn't keep door-keys on key-rings.'

'Blast you, Gently!' exploded the super. He turned on Hansom viciously. 'What sort of a bloody policeman are you? Go in there and find that key – and don't come out till you've got it!' He turned back to Gently. 'All right – so if it isn't there you've made a point – but you haven't proved your case or anything like it. Meantime I'm giving the Coroner's Court the OK and this case is going in on its merits. I'm satisfied with what I've got. If you want more, you'd better go after it – only you won't be getting any help from me. Is that clear?'

Gently felt sadly in his pocket and brought out an empty bag. 'Quite clear,' he said, screwing it into a ball, 'quite clear.'

CHAPTER FOURTEEN

THE CORONER'S COURT sat on the day following and returned on Nicholas Huysmann a verdict of death resulting from a stab wound inflicted by his chauffeur, James Fisher, and on his chauffeur a verdict of *felo de se*. Chief Inspector Gently, Central Office, CID, gave immaculate evidence and was publicly congratulated by the Coroner both for this and for his ready assistance, although on holiday. Superintendent Walker and the Norchester Police, CID, also came in for congratulations.

The super muttered grimly as they left the court: 'You given up this Leaming business then?'

Gently smiled and shook his head.

'Thanks for letting it ride, anyway.'

Gently shrugged, but as he turned away the super caught his arm. 'I didn't mean quite all I said last night . . . I'd like you to keep me posted. And if you need any help – within reason, of course.'

Peter Huysmann had been released the evening before, the charge against him dropped out of hand. He had been at court, slightly dazed by his sudden return to the world, but had only been required to testify to the accuracy of his statement, which was then read for him. For the time being he was continuing to live at the caravan, where he had been received with much rejoicing and congratulation by his late boss and by the fair community in general. It was considered a signal victory over the auld enemy . . .

Rejoicing there was also at Charlie's, for Charlie had come to look on the 'getting' of Fisher as almost a personal issue. 'I knew it was him from the start,' he told a group of lorry-drivers, 'right from the time Chief Inspector Gently first come in here, I could smell what was in the wind. Ah, he's a foxy one, he is! He just let the City Police go on thinking it was young Huysmann and then when they got their hands on him, "No," he says, "you let young Huysmann be. Just give me twenty-four hours," he says, "and I'll have the one you want!" Ah, he played with Fisher like a cat with a mouse. Fisher, he thinks he's this and he thinks he's that . . . but all the time the Chief Inspector was getting nearer and nearer to him, taking his time, never in a hurry, till last of all even Fisher can see that the game is up . . . well, there you are. There was only two ways out, and he took the handiest . . .'

Gretchen, subdued, bowed, dressed entirely in black, with a veil which hid any expression in her waxen face, had also made a statement which was read for her in court. It had been drafted by Gently and was exquisite in its restraint. At the point where the hiding of the knife was described the Coroner was moved to raise his glasses and deliver a look of reproof, but a closer view of the dark-clad figure decided him to let the matter rest. With Susan, on the other hand, he was positively genial.

Late final editions carried a full report of the inquest, were scanned perfunctorily in cafés and snack-bars and on the crowded buses carrying city workers back to the suburbs. It was a satisfactory but tame dénouement. The affair had raised expectations of a hard-fought trial with all the exciting trappings of judicial slaying . . . quite a fair stretch of innocent entertainment. As the clerk at Simmonds said to Miss Jones (blouses), 'You can't get really worked up over a thing like that. But if it had been the son, now . . .' 'Bloody flash in the pan *that* was,' said a news-vendor, 'thank God for the football, that's what I say.'

Inspector Hansom went about his duties, a wounded soul. He hadn't had much sleep. Into the small hours of the morning he had been at Fisher's flat and, at the super's suggestion, all the area within a key's throw of the flat, searching for the blasted key that had to be there and wasn't . . . as dawn had begun to show far off down the Yar valley he had been assailed by unpolicemanlike thoughts. There was a firm in the city who would turn out an identical key for a couple of bob . . . and wasn't it worth a couple of bob to get one's head down? At the same time, if that key really was missing . . . and you had to admit that Gently was a clever bastard . . . Hansom lit a bad-tasting cigar and breathed expensively towards the dawn.

Leaming, well-dressed and impressive, had given his brief evidence to the court with precision and conviction. One felt that here was a man of ability, a man who could handle affairs of moment: a man to be trusted implicitly. The Coroner treated him with deference. As he concluded his short statement he glanced round the court and catching Gently's eye, smiled to him winningly. Gently smiled also, but it would have been more difficult to categorize Gently's smile.

A police car still stood in Paradise Alley, lone and smart amongst the derelict houses and blank, shabby walls. Gently nodded to the constable who stood by it.

'Have they had any luck?'

'Not so far, sir, but they're just taking the floor up.'

Gently clicked his tongue. 'They won't find it there.'

'There's a crack where it might have slipped through, sir . . . they've found the head off an old hammer and a threepenny bit.'

'Well . . . tell them not to spend it all at once.'

'Ha, ha! Yes, sir.'

Gently turned away to the row of empty windows opposite. No fierce little head bobbed up to greet him, but then, it was probably Superman's bedtime. He shoved open a yawing door and went through. The floor above had caved in long since, leaving a rusty fireplace hanging on the wall in heartless nakedness. The back of the house was a collapsed pile of rubble. Gently climbed over it and looked down at the desolation below. Walls disintegrating, sagging roofs, piles of rubble surmounted by nettles and ragwort . . . right down to Queen Street, where the shabby thoroughfare arrested the ruins with a narrow bulwark of vitality. He shook his head and picked his way cautiously through a fragment-strewn yard.

'Gotcher!' rang out a triumphant shout behind him. Gently put up his hands and came to a standstill. 'Turn around!' commanded the voice, 'and don't try any funny stuff on the Cactus Kid!' Gently turned around. 'Oh . . . it's you, mister . . .'

Gently nodded. 'Yes, it's me . . . can I put my hands down?'

Superman, alias the Cactus Kid, wrinkled his nose in a frown. 'Guess you can, mister . . . though you look mighty like Bad Dan from behind. He's the worsest rustler that ever hit these parts, and I'm sure going to get him one of these days!'

'It's time you hit the hay,' said Gently, lowering his hands, 'there's a sheriff's posse up the alley. They'll keep watch out for Bad Dan till you get on the trail again. You come along back to the ranch with me.' He took the Cactus Kid's grimy paw and led the way round a lurching segment of wall towards Mariner's Lane. 'This is heap bad country, pardner,' he added, 'you should find up a better range somewhere . . .'

The Cactus Kid trotted along beside him happily. 'Mister, they got on to Red Hawk at last . . . I knew about him a long time ago. Did they find all the gold he'd got hidden away?'

'Guess they did, kid.'

'Gee, mister, that must've been exciting!'

'Waal . . . it had its moments.'

'I sure do wish I'd been around about then.'

Gently looked down at his small companion. 'Weren't you up here yesterday?' he asked.

'No, mister, not me.'

'How come, pardner?'

'Someone gave me two bob to spend on the fair . . . but it wasn't going in the afternoon. So I went round Woolies instead. That's where I bought my six-shooter, mister – see here!' He withdrew his hand from Gently's and held up a new toy gun. Gently examined it gravely, spinning the magazine with a stubby finger. 'Clean, bright and lightly oiled,' he murmured, 'that's a pretty little shooting-iron, pardner . . . here's half a buck to buy it some ammo.'

'Gee . . . mister!' The Cactus Kid's eyes gleamed as he felt the heavy coin with its rough milled edge. Then he tugged back on Gently's hand. 'Mister . . . would you mind if I spent some of it on a special belt with a holster?'

They came down Mariner's Lane, Gently instinctively steering outwards at the spot where the masonry had been aimed at him. Queen Street was lit dully in the twilight. Across the way the Huysmann house reared more blankly and detachedly than ever, white and looming in the blueness of a mercury lamp. 'Whereabouts is your bunk-house, pardner?' enquired Gently.

'Just here, mister – one of those in the row.'

Gently paused in the act of dismissing him. 'Who gave you the two bob yesterday?' he queried.

'Oh, it was a man.'

'Somebody you know?'

'No . . . he wasn't anybody. He came down the Lane when I was keeping watch on Red Hawk.'

'When was that?'

'I don't know . . . it wasn't tea-time.'

'Coming *down* the lane, was he?'

'That's right, mister. I was just on the corner there, keeping watch down the alley. He give me the two bob to go on the fair . . . only it wasn't going in the afternoon.'

Gently bent closer to the little freckled face. 'This man, what was he like?'

'He was just a man . . .'

'Did you notice if he was carrying a bag?'

'That's right, mister – he'd got a bag, one of those bulgy ones.'

'And did he go up the alley?'

'I don't know . . . he might have done.'

Gently stood back again, brooding, gazing into the far distance towards Railway Bridge. The Cactus Kid fidgeted from one foot to the other. 'It wasn't anyone, mister . . . it was just a man.'

'Which way did you go to the fairground?' asked Gently abruptly.

'I went up the lane and along the top . . . but it wasn't going.'

'Did you see a racing car standing at the top – a real fast one, painted red?'

'One that could go a hundred miles an hour?'

'About that . . . maybe faster.'

'Oh yes, I saw that one, mister – it had got an aeroplane on the front – I blew the propeller round!'

A slow smile spread over Gently's face and he felt in his pocket for his bag of peppermint creams. 'Here,' he said, 'take the lot . . . but don't eat them all tonight or you'll have nightmares. There's just one other thing before you go . . . I suppose you haven't found a key up there round the alley?'

The Cactus Kid shook his head vigorously.

'Ah!' sighed Gently, 'we mustn't strain providence too far, must we, pardner?'

The front doorbell of the Huysmann house was engulfed afar off, giving back to the ringer not the faintest vibration to encourage him in his practices: one rang, and waited unhopefully. Eventually Gently heard the soft pad of feet down the hall and the shooting of the bolt. It was Susan who melted in the doorway.

'Oh, Inspector . . .!'

Gently remained on the step. 'I just want some information,' he said.

Susan's blue eyes chided him softly. 'Won't you come in, Inspector? Miss Gretchen has gone to bed, and Mrs Turner has gone to tell her sister about everything . . . it's lonely in here, on your own.'

'I don't think I'll come in at the moment . . .'

'Inspector, I thought you were *wonderful* in court . . . absolutely *wonderful*.'

'Thank you, my dear . . . I've had considerable experience.'

'The way you stood up there in front of them all – so cool and strong – ohh! It just *did* something to me!'

'I hope it was nothing irremediable. Now, my dear—'

'You're sure you won't come in . . . just for a little while?'

Gently sighed. 'I'm *busy*,' he said.

'Oh . . . I see.' Susan's face fell. 'We-ell . . . what did you want to know?'

'I want to know where I'm likely to find Mr Leaming.'

'Him! I s'pose he's gone home.'

'He didn't strike me as the home-loving kind . . . I thought he might be around in the city.'

'Well, he might have gone to a show . . . or he might be at the Venetian. He used to go there a lot.'

'Is that the place near the Castle?'

'That's right. It's a classy sort of place with an orchestra. He was always one to flash his money about.'

'Thank you, my dear . . . you've always been a great help.'

Susan's eyes swam up to him. 'It'd be so nice to have someone to talk to for a bit.'

But Gently had gone.

The Venetian Club was underground, beneath one of the larger and more expensive hotels. One reached it by a long, wide, sweeping stairway with a rail supported on criss-cross steel rods, painted maroon and ivory. Below was a large floor, open in the centre for dancing, carpeted at the sides with deep-pile carpet, also maroon. At the far end was the orchestra rostrum, and on the right the bar. Down each side and along the top ran the tables, glass tops on criss-cross ivory legs, spaced out with tubs of ferns and an occasional settee upholstered in ivory leather. The lighting was soft and diffused. There was an atmosphere of leisured peace and timelessness.

Gently left his coat and trilby upstairs, went jerkily down the stairway, aware of the out-of-placeness of his rather shabbily dressed, heavy figure. He knew Leaming was there. He had seen the vermilion Pashley parked just over the way. Near the foot of the stairs he paused to run his eye over the floor, table by table. Leaming was seated by himself not far from the bar, eating, a bottle of champagne in ice beside him, his back half-turned to the stairs. Gently continued down the stairs.

'A single table, sir?' The head waiter looked down his nose at the incongruous arrival.

'I'll take that one over there,' said Gently, pointing to a table near the wall at the side opposite to where Leaming sat. The head waiter ushered him across and he seated himself heavily in a padded, criss-cross chair. Another waiter slid into position at his elbow. Gently grabbed the menu and examined it, frowning. 'Bring me a coffee,' he said.

There was a pregnant interval. '. . . *only* a coffee, sir?' queried the waiter.

Gently turned slowly about and faced him. '*Only* a coffee,' he said.

The waiter wilted. 'Very good, sir . . . a coffee.'

Gently lapsed back into his chair and tossed the menu aside. The orchestra was playing its pale, emasculated semblance of music, obviously not to be listened to, and two or three couples on the floor were obviously not listening to it: the rhythm alone guiding their sauntered steps. On Gently's right an elderly man in evening dress sat with his wife. They were silently eating asparagus and drinking white wine. On his left, partly obscured by a tub of ferns, sat a party of four, rather noisy, busily attended by two waiters.

'My dear, I thought it was because Gerald wasn't coming . . .'

'Did you really think he wouldn't come . . . I mean, did you?'

'Well, I mean, under the circs . . .'

'Tony sounds as though he knows more about it than we do . . . my dear, it's just possible that he *does*!'

Followed by laughter.

Gently received his coffee in a small, exquisite cup. Across the way a waiter was pouring out Leaming's champagne. Leaming seemed to be cracking a joke with him about something, and they both laughed as Leaming took the filled glass and the waiter returned the bottle to its ice. Leaming was having a little celebration, no doubt. As he lifted the glass, Gently caught his eye. Leaming hesitated a brief second, the glass poised and winking: then he drank it off, turning again to the waiter and laughing.

Gently stirred several lumps of sugar into his inadequate cup. Leaming didn't look his way again. Handsome, smiling, polished, well-dressed, the manager of Huysmann's fitted the picture as though he were made to measure. The waiters admired him, the management rejoiced in his patronage . . . and 'He was always one to flash his money about.' Yes, there was no doubt that Leaming fitted the picture.

He had got to his cigar now. As the waiter lit it for him, Leaming took the waiter's pad and scribbled something on it and sent him off with a motion of his head. Gently watched the waiter threading his way through the tables with bland indifference.

'Well?' he demanded.

The waiter made a slight bow. 'The gentleman at table seven sends you this note, sir.'

Gently took it. It read: 'Join me in celebrating your success.' He took out his wallet and ostentatiously folded the note into it. 'Give my regrets to the gentleman at table seven and tell him I'm here on business,' he said.

The waiter bowed again and departed. Out of the corner of his eye Gently watched him gliding back between the tables. Leaming received his message with a shrug of his elegant shoulders, laughed, and pushed forward his glass for more champagne. But the sparkle had gone out of him now. The laughs were a little forced and came between intervals of brooding over his cigar, over his glass. Once or twice he tried to catch Gently's eye, but each time Gently was resolutely looking in some other direction, or drinking his coffee. He never seemed to be looking at Leaming. He was just there, a dark, remorseless presence.

Leaming called for the evening paper and read it, frowning. It contained a full account of the inquest. There, with complete finality, the Huysmann case was dissected, analysed, judged and put away . . . solved and dismissed. Everyone had been satisfied. Yet there sat Gently like the Old Man of the Sea, clinging, watching, unshakable in his obstinacy, a ratiocinating limpet who refused to be given the slip. What did the stupid little man think he could do now?

The band was playing a popular hit tune of the moment. Several couples got up to dance. A woman Leaming knew came over to his table, gushing, looking for a partner.

'Darling! I didn't know you were here all alone . . .'

'I just looked in for a bite to eat . . .'

'Oh, but you simply must dance this one with me!'

'I couldn't, Laura . . . too soon after dinner.'

'Just the teeniest weeniest hop, darling?'

'Look – there's Geoffrey Davis over there . . . rouse him out for a dance.'

He was staring at Gently more directly now, trying to catch him out. But Gently was not to be caught. The only indication he gave that he was interested in Leaming was that he never looked at him. Now, he was ordering another cup of coffee. With the waiter standing before him, his eyes had only to slip a fraction to one side for a glance at Leaming, yet they firmly refused to make that slip. It was silly, childish . . . like a schoolboy game. He became suddenly furious with Gently. If the man was there to watch him, why didn't he watch him, instead of playing the fool like this? How much longer would he sit there, drinking coffee at one-and-six a cup?

Gently was beginning to wonder about that himself, though with such small cups it represented no hardship, and the coffee was quite good. He was getting hungry, of course . . . but the Venetian's menu had been drawn up for Chief Constables rather than Chief Inspectors. So he toyed with an empty pipe instead. Dancing had become more general now and there was a steady trickle of new arrivals. Supper was being served to the tables all round him. A younger and more romantic couple had taken the table previously occupied by the asparagus-eaters, a callow young man cutting loose with his boss's secretary, perhaps.

At eleven fifteen Leaming paid his bill with two five-pound notes, waiving the change. Gently made no move as he left his table and sauntered casually towards the foot of the stairs. There he paused to light a cigarette. The gold cigarette case opened and closed with a distant snap, and a waiter appeared from nowhere with a lighter. Leaming stood with his head bowed, apparently in thought. Then, as though remembering something, he raised his head with a smile and slipped across to the table where Gently was sitting.

'You run to late hours in your business?' he said brightly.

Gently eyed him without expression. 'It depends on our clients . . . some of them never go to bed.'

Leaming took the seat opposite. 'I thought you were down here on holiday . . . naturally, since our business was cleared up, I didn't expect to find you engaged in something fresh.'

'I'm not.'

'Not on something fresh?'

'No.'

Leaming looked at him uncomprehendingly. 'But I thought this thing came to an end at the inquest . . . there doesn't seem much left to explain.'

'Some things come to an end at inquests, but this isn't one of them.'

'Well . . . if I can assist you in any way, don't be afraid to ask. If it's some silly little complication to do with the firm I dare say I can put you straight.'

Gently rocked a little in his chair. 'It concerns the main issue,' he said, 'the person Fisher saw stabbing Huysmann . . . and the person who cut Fisher's throat subsequently.' His green eyes fixed on Leaming, still completely without expression.

Leaming remained silent, taut, cigarette angled from the corner of his mouth.

'That doesn't surprise you?' enquired Gently, with a trace of sarcasm.

'Yes . . . it does.'

'You'd like to make a statement about it?'

Leaming's eyes met his, brown and powerful, cautious as a wild animal's: they broke into a smile. 'Why should I make a statement about it?'

Gently shook his head, as though acknowledging the point. 'Would you like to tell me how you spent yesterday afternoon?'

'I'd love to . . . where do you want me to start?'

'Start where you dropped me after lunch.'

'Very well. I went to the office and looked through the afternoon mail . . . then I dictated some letters . . . then I took some specifications over to Sainty's the contractors.' Leaming paused, mockingly. 'I was gone about an hour,' he added.

'And the time?'

'Ah . . . the time. I felt that would be important. Well, I left the office at half-past three and re-entered it at twenty-six and a half minutes to five.'

'And you were at Sainty's during all that time?'

'Dear me, no – only for about twenty minutes.'

'Where were you during the remainder of that time?'

Leaming's smile came back, strong, confident, almost reproving. 'Oh, just driving around, you know. I've got a nice car. I get a kick out of negotiating the traffic with it.'

'And that's your official story?'

'Yes, I think so . . . unless somebody can give me a reason for putting out a better one.'

Gently nodded, keeping his eyes fixed on Leaming's. 'Suppose I say that the little boy to whom you gave two shillings saw your car parked in Burgh Street . . . would that be reason enough?'

'There's a lot of cars get parked in Burgh Street.'

'But this one was a red sports car . . . it had an aeroplane mascot. The little boy blew the propeller round. Also, it was parked near Mariner's Lane.'

There was a pause, charged and vibrant. The smile still flickered in Leaming's eyes. 'No,' he said at last, 'I don't think it is. Somehow, I've never relied very much on little boys as witnesses . . . have you? They forget things so easily . . . they rarely make a convincing impression. No, I'll stick to my story.'

Gently said: 'Then there's the bag . . .'

Leaming made no response.

'The gladstone bag that had the money in it, the bag that Fisher was bending over when his throat was cut.' He leaned forward, his eyes boring at Leaming's compellingly. But Leaming met them, hard and impenetrable. There was no give in him at all.

'So it was a gladstone bag?'

'Yes, a gladstone bag. And during the murder it got bloodied . . . so did some of the notes which were lying on top. The blood was wiped off the bag temporarily, but one can't get rid of blood as easily as that – not so that it becomes undetectable in laboratory tests – so the bag had to be destroyed.'

'Go on,' said Leaming, 'you're interesting me.'

'This evening, just before I came up here, I stepped into the timber-yard for a moment.'

'Well . . . I hope everything was in order . . .'

'I noticed a fire smouldering in a corner near the quays, so I went over and had a look at it. It was the remains of a large, sawdust-rubbish fire, apparently one that is kept burning there almost continuously . . .'

'You make a good detective.'

'. . . and after stirring it about a little I came across two interesting items. One of them was the handle-frame of a gladstone bag . . . and the other was the key to Fisher's flat. They were both together in one part of the fire, which suggested to me that the key had been in the bag at the time it was introduced into the fire. The murderer, it seems, had forgotten to take it out . . . which was certainly a mistake, don't you think?'

The stare of Leaming's eyes never wavered. 'It could have been chucked in the river, I suppose.'

'I think that would have been safer.'

'At the same time, there's nothing to connect it with any one person.'

'Oh yes . . . there's the maker's name on the handle-frame, and what may be a serial number on the lock. A little routine work should indicate the owner to us.'

Leaming shook his head slowly. 'It won't do, you know, it isn't a clincher. There've been dozens of those bags sold, and the number on the lock is merely a convenience, in case you lose the key. Nobody keeps a record correlating it with the purchaser.'

'Nevertheless, it will be useful to show that a certain person was the owner of such a bag. It's surprising how points like that increase in significance when taken with other points.'

The smile glided back into Leaming's eyes. 'They might, if you could arrange them convincingly . . . but you've first to convince the authorities that Fisher was murdered at all. At the moment their considered opinion is that he wasn't . . . we mustn't forget that, must we? If you go to them saying, "There's a case against A for murdering Fisher," they will simply look blank and say, "But Fisher wasn't murdered." And what have you got to say to that?'

Leaming leaned back in his chair, his eyes lit and triumphant. Gently sat still and unmoved, one stubby hand clasped in the other.

'Of course, you could talk about finding the handle-frame and the key,' continued Leaming, 'you could tell them all about your imaginative idea of somebody taking Fisher the money in that bag, of how Fisher was murdered over it and how the bag would then have to be destroyed. But how would you set about proving it? And as for the key, they might want to know if there couldn't have been two of them – there usually is, isn't there? – and how can you be sure that the one you found was the one that a murderer locked the flat with? Well, I don't know what you could say to that, but if they asked me . . .'

'Yes,' breathed Gently, 'and if they asked you?'

'. . . I should say that the key was most probably Fisher's spare, and that the bag was an old one that I had given him at some time.'

Leaming broke off, pleasantly, as though intrigued by an interesting speculation.

'And how about the key which wasn't Fisher's spare?'

Leaming shrugged his shoulders gracefully. 'It's a little puzzling, of course. But the fact that it was missing didn't seem to affect things much at the inquest . . . it was such a small point, after all, when the rest of the evidence was so irresistible.' He leaned right back, tilting the chair, quizzing Gently.

Gently twisted his one hand in the other. 'You seem to have given this matter a lot of thought . . .' he said.

'I try to help the police to the best of my ability.'

'There's just one thing, though.'

Leaming's eyebrows lifted, almost negligently. 'Something I've overlooked?'

'You may not have overlooked it, but at the same time you may not have realized its full significance.'

'Go on,' said Leaming.

Gently spread his clumsy hands wide open on the top of the table. 'The case that's building up against Fisher's murderer may be good, may be bad . . . that's something

219

we shall both find out. But if anything should turn up to suggest that Fisher may not have been the one to kill Huysmann, then that case is going to spring to life overnight.'

Leaming leaned forward off his chair. 'Such as?' he demanded.

'Such as somebody's alibi springing a leak.'

Leaming went back again, slowly, thoughtfully, the smile grown thin on his face. 'There's that, of course . . .' he admitted softly, 'there's always a possibility of an alibi being cracked.'

Gently rose to his feet and beckoned to a waiter. 'It's getting late . . . I suppose you're just going?'

Leaming looked up at him lazily. 'I may go – I may stay on.'

'I'll pay my bill at all events . . . then I'll be ready, whichever you decide to do.'

CHAPTER FIFTEEN

G ENTLY HAD RARELY felt so checkmated as he did during the next two days. It was true that the super's interest had been well and truly roused by the discovery of the key and the handle-frame, but cautious as ever, he had scented all the difficulties that still remained before a credible case could be made out. The main weakness, he pointed out, was Gently's inability to prove a motive. He could produce no evidence to show that Fisher had been blackmailing Leaming. Without such evidence, there was no logical connection between the handle-frame and Fisher's death, and hence with Leaming. He agreed that Gently was being very convincing and that he appeared to be on a trail. But Gently had to remember that their own medico ruled out the possibility of murder and he, the super, still felt most inclined to support that viewpoint.

In other words, he thought that Gently had a bee in his bonnet.

Glumly Gently went back over the trail, checking and re-checking, asking the same questions again and getting substantially the same answers. He cornered the tug-skipper in Charlie's and gave him a grilling, but he would scarcely open his mouth. The 'Straight Grain' people had packed up, he said, they weren't taking any more deliveries. No, he didn't know where their place had been. No, they didn't own the quay . . . it was derelict. Anybody could use it.

Pursuing this line, Gently went down to the quay itself. There was no doubt about its dereliction. Sited between tumble-down warehouses, its rotting piles formed just enough staithe to moor a single barge. Once there had been a shallow pent roof over it, but of this there remained only a couple of beams, dangerous, decorated with willow-herb, and on each side of the run-in to the quay nettles and ragwort cropped hectically. The place was deserted. Gently hailed an old fellow who was tinkering with a hauled-out rowing boat further down the bank. 'Hi! . . . do you know who owns this place?'

The old man put down a can of varnish and came limping along to the dividing fence. He looked Gently over without interest. 'There int nobody what own it,' he said.

Gently pointed to the piling. 'Somebody must have owned it at some time.'

'Well, there was old Thrower had it . . . thirty odd year ago. But he never owned it neither. He just come and built that there staithe, and nobody said nothin' to him, but he never rightly owned it.'

'And where is Thrower now?'

'Dead . . . thirty odd year ago.'

Gently sighed. 'I suppose you don't know anything about the people who've been using it lately?'

'No, I don't know nothin' about them.'

Of course, if the super would put a fraud man on the books and use his resources for a general check-up, thought Gently bitterly . . . but then again, suppose they *could* bring it home to Leaming – there was still nothing to tie Leaming to the main issue. Works managers have feathered their nests before today without necessarily bumping off the proprietor. No: it was no use chasing side-issues. Once a charge was laid, the details would be ferreted out by routine work. And if the charge wasn't laid, then the details might just as well be forgotten.

Leaving nothing to chance, he plodded across to the Railway Road Football Ground. The car park was as Leaming had described it, between the south end of the ground and the river. There was no direct entry from the park to the ground. One had to return to the road and enter by the turnstiles or by the stand. The surface of the park was cinder-dirt, worn rather thin – dry now, but with plenty of clayey depressions where puddles had been not so long since. Gently came out and went into the ground through the main stand entrance. Nobody enquired his business. Two groundsmen were working in one of the goal-mouths, a third was driving a motor-roller, while three or four City players in tracksuits jog-trotted round the running track. Gently strolled out on to the pitch to where the groundsmen were working. 'Do you know where I can find the car park attendants?' he asked.

One of the groundsmen straightened up and surveyed him coolly. 'Who wants to know?' he countered.

'Police.'

'Why – what's wrong now?'

Gently shook his head sadly. 'I just want some information . . . that's all.'

'What do you want to know?'

'Are you one of the attendants?'

The groundsman twisted his mouth and spat. 'I could be,' he said.

'Were you on the park last Saturday?'

'Suppose I was?'

Gently held out his hand in a gesture of non-aggression. 'I'm not trying to pinch anyone . . . I just want to know something. Do you remember a red Pashley sports with an aeroplane mascot being parked there?'

'You mean Mr Leaming's car?'

'That's right – do you know him?'

'I should do. He's there often enough.'

'And his car was there?'

'Yep.'

Gently paused, comfortably. 'Whenabouts did it check in?' he proceeded.

'I dunno . . . just before the match.'

'Did Mr Leaming say or do anything that he didn't usually say or do?'

'Well . . .' The groundsman looked puzzledly at Gently, trying to decide what was behind it all. 'He talked to me about the team changes and such-like. He don't do that as a rule, I suppose, and then again, it was just on kick-off.'

'Did you see him enter the ground?'

'I'd got other things to do besides watch him.'

'Were you there when he collected his car?'

'Yep.'

'About when was that?'

'Same time as all the others.'

'He wasn't there a little early, by any chance?'

'Not so's you'd notice it . . . he may've been ahead of the rush.'

'Thank you,' said Gently, 'that seems to be everything.'

Outside in Railway Road he stood looking back at the ground. There lay the secret, the missing link . . . if only he could get his hands on it. Someone in there, or someone who had been in there on Saturday, could supply it. Someone who knew Leaming. Someone who could testify that he hadn't been at the match . . . even someone who had seen him double back over Railway Bridge. But how did one separate that someone from the other twenty-nine thousand, nine hundred and ninety-nine?

His eye fell on the little glass box perched on the side of Railway Bridge. The bridge-keeper! A gleam came into Gently's eye. Was it his lucky day . . . was his detective's guardian angel keeping this one up his sleeve for him?

'Police,' he said simply. 'Were you on duty here last Saturday afternoon?'

The bridge-keeper stared at him. 'W'yes . . .' he said.

'Do you know Huysmann's manager, Leaming, by sight?'

'Mr Leaming? Yes, I know him.'

'Did you see him crossing the bridge in this direction just about the time the match started on Saturday?'

The bridge-keeper frowned and rubbed the side of his chin. 'There was a powerful crowd of people going over the bridge about then . . . I don't suppose I'd have seen him anyway.'

'Later on . . . between four and five . . . did you see him come back again?'

The bridge-keeper brightened up. 'Oh no, sir –
I couldn't have done. We close down here at half-past
three on a Saturday . . . the bridge don't open again till
Monday morning.'

It was the same wherever he went. There was plenty
of fuel for his moral certainty, but the cold, hard proof
eluded every enquiry. Grudgingly, he had to admire the
manager of Huysmann's for his crisp, sure performance.
It had needed luck, and Leaming had had luck . . . but,
with Sempronius, he had deserved it.

Dispirited, Gently made his way down Queen Street
to Charlie's. He had no real purpose in going there. It was
rather a piece of conditioned behaviour – Charlie's had
been useful before, so he turned to it now when he was
at a loose end. Outside stood the usual trucks and vans,
and from the yard across the way came the familiar
accompaniment of screaming and whining. Leaming's
world, going full tilt.

But Leaming himself was in Charlie's. He was standing
at the bar eating a sandwich, nonchalant, aware of himself
as being of a different creation from his surroundings. He
smiled brightly as Gently entered.

'Still busy?' he remarked, tentatively.

Gently glanced at him and grunted. Then he pushed to
the bar, ignoring him, and called for a cup of tea. The
ghost of a frown appeared on Leaming's brow. He turned
towards Gently confidentially, as though expecting a
conversation to start. But Gently, having received his tea,
went away to a table and began sipping it as though
Leaming didn't exist. Charlie watched this little by-play
with interest; leant across, and whispered: 'He's on to
something – you mark my words!'

Leaming lifted a patronizing eyebrow. 'How do you know?'

'I seen him like that before . . . and you know what happened that time.'

Leaming shrugged contemptuously. 'Don't judge strangers so hastily . . . the Inspector is merely feeling tired.' He went over to where Gently sat. 'You look fed up,' he said, 'haven't things turned out as well as you hoped for?'

Still Gently refused to look at him. The slight, lacing edge of anxiety in Leaming's tone was like music. It reassured Gently. It told him that Leaming was getting worried, that the strain was beginning to tell on him. The heat should have been off by now . . . and it wasn't. Gently was still after him. And though he could tell himself that he held the trump cards, yet always there must be that little element of doubt, that tiny risk of something turning up . . . Even the fed-up look of Gently's was suspect. It might be assumed to lull Leaming into a deceptive sense of security.

Gently sensed this, and smiled inwardly. His labours had not been completely in vain. Leaming was tough and cool and clever, but there was a limit to him: Gently could feel the initiative beginning to pass into his hands.

'I've just come from the football ground,' he said to his tea-cup.

Leaming laughed, but his laugh betrayed no nervousness. 'I hope they're getting into good trim for the match tomorrow.'

'I was talking to the car park attendant.'

'Which one – the red-haired fellow?'

'This one had brown hair and grey eyes and small ears that stuck out.'

'Oh, you mean Dusty.' Leaming grinned, as though to excuse his familiarity. 'He's quite knowledgeable on football matters – I had a chat with him myself the other day.'

'So he was telling me.'

'Indeed?'

'Just as the match was starting, too. I think it surprised him that you should stop to talk football, when you were already late.' Gently turned slowly and fixed his green eyes on Leaming's.

'Oh, he's probably exaggerating. On Saturday, I only had a couple of words with him.'

'It sounded like more than that, the way he told it.'

'Well . . . with a policeman chivvying him and putting ideas into his head . . . but it's quite true that I chatted to him as he was sticking a chit under my windscreen-wiper.'

Gently nodded with a sort of vague satisfaction, as though the answer was just what he wished. 'And as I was coming over the bridge I spoke to the bridge-keeper.'

'You mean . . . Railway Bridge?'

'That's right. I don't know which one, but he knows you . . . by sight.'

The tenseness now was visible in Leaming's face. He stared into Gently's eyes as though he would reach down and pluck out the knowledge that might be lurking there. 'You mean the one with glasses,' he said quickly, 'he's so short-sighted that he can scarcely read his time-sheets . . . he ought not to be on that job at all.'

'He didn't complain of short-sightedness to me.'

'Naturally – he doesn't want to lose his post.'

'I don't even remember the glasses.'

'He tries not to wear them when there's anybody about.'

Gently picked up his cup and took a long, reflective sip. 'What makes you think it was the short-sighted one I was talking to?' he enquired affably.

Leaming hesitated. 'I noticed he was on as I came by after lunch . . . in any case, he's the only one who knows me.'

'Would you say he was the one who was on duty last Saturday?'

'God knows – didn't you ask him?'

Gently shrugged and said nothing.

'Did he tell you that they packed up at half-past three on Saturdays?'

'He might have done.'

Leaming leaned back, away from the table. Gently could see one brown hand tighten till there was whiteness about the knuckles. Then slowly it relaxed, the long, sensitive fingers uncurling, the thumb pointing outwards as Leaming forced calmness on himself. 'You should be on that bridge when a match is on . . . there can be several hundred people a minute going over it.'

'That's a lot of people . . . all going one way.'

'And the boys selling programmes and football publications, all crowded round with their customers . . . just in front of the bridge-keeper's box.'

'You're making it sound quite busy.'

'If you don't believe me – tomorrow's Saturday – go and look for yourself.'

Gently puckered his mouth ruminatively. 'I may do that,' he said, 'yes . . . I may do that. I hear it's going to be a good match, against the Cobblers.'

* * *

Norchester on a football Saturday woke up from the even tenor of its week-days. Soon after eleven o'clock the coaches began to stream into the city, coaches from the distantmost parts of Northshire – for the City had a big county following – and even from further afield. Out of the brooding depths of Thorne Station poured crowds of supporters with their rattles and gay favours of yellow and green, and the streets were thronged at lunch-time with factory-workers. The little cheap cafés and snack-bars did a roaring trade. Charlie's, for instance, took on two extra hands for football Saturdays.

Riverside and Queen Street were the two main arteries from the city. Riverside, wide, tree-lined, with a long, broad flank between itself and the river, took the coach traffic: it had brightly painted vehicles parked three or four deep, so close to the edge of the quay that passengers were obliged to dismount from one side only. Queen Street, narrow and close-set, took the crowds from the city centre. Also it took the cyclists – for whom, at the far end, an insistent body of Queen Streeters touted their cycle-parks. At Railway Bridge the seething current from the city was joined by the rushing stream from Bracken-dale and together they poured over the bridge, a bridge that trembled beneath their thousand feet. Small wonder that Leaming was sceptical about being seen by the bridge-keeper, thought Gently.

He himself passed over quite close to the little glass box, staring hard at its inmate as he went by. But the bridge-keeper was apparently bored by football crowds. He sat with his back to them, reading the midday paper.

On the other side of the bridge the crush was again augmented by the disemboguing of Riverside. Gently was hustled down like a cork. He barely had time to glance across at the car park with its tangle of moving and stationary vehicles when he was swept past and left high and dry on the end of a turnstile queue. How could one man be singled out in all that turmoil . . .? One had enough to do looking after oneself. If this had been last Saturday, would he, Gently, have noticed which way Leaming had gone when he left the car park . . . or even if Leaming was there at all?

The queue behind thrust him through the absurdly narrow little turnstile like a pip coming out of an orange, his one-and-nine snatched from his hand. He found himself amongst the loose, running crowd at the back of the terraces. Already the terraces seemed full, thronged with a dark, mass of humanity, a strange livid weal. But they were not full yet, because the armies still marched over Railway Bridge, still hurried down Queen Street, Riverside, and at the far end, down Railway Road. Thirty thousand people, perhaps more. Gently made his way round to the far side, the popular side, and forgetting he was no longer a uniform man, shouldered his way pretty well to the front.

Opposite him stretched the grandstand, all the length of the pitch, in front the packed enclosure, behind the close-banked tiers of seats, rising into the interior gloom, fully fledged with their human freight. On his right reared the Barclay stand, not seated, airier and less boxed-in than the other. Ice-cream boys marched along the naming-track. They caught sixpences with unerring hands and hurled their wares far up into the murmuring crowd. In the centre of the pitch tossed a bunch of balloons in the opposing colours . . . the City's flag hung palely after nearly a season's rains.

Gently leaned on the corner of a crush-rail and took it in, section by section. It was here, if he could find it, there was something here that would give Leaming's alibi the lie . . . something. But what was it, that something? How could he abstract it from a pattern so large and over-whelming? The loud-speaker music broke out in a strident, remorseless march, overriding his thought and concentration, compelling him to accept it, to accept the occasion, to accept the mood of the crowd . . . he shook his head and went on searching. It was here, he repeated to himself, almost like a spell.

The match went well for the City. Not always immaculate before their own crowd, they took command of the game from the kick-off and rarely let it out of their grasp till the final whistle. Yet there was very little excitement. The score, two-one, indicated a hard-fought battle, whereas if the City had taken all their chances they might have gone near double figures. The crowd was correspondingly apathetic, seeing their team so near a resounding victory and still unable to force it home.

'We ought to have had Cullis here today . . . he'd've shown them where the goal was. Alfie wants to have everything laid on for him.'

'Lord knows how Noel missed that last one.'

'I reckon Ken is standing in the goal there, laughing at them.'

A particularly glaring miss was acknowledged by a slow hand-clap from one section of the crowd. When the final whistle went there was very little ovation for either side. Immediately the spectators turned and began their shuffle towards the exits, dissatisfied, feeling it might have been much better than it was.

'Well,' said one pundit to his mate, 'at least it was a *clean* game . . . they weren't like that lot we had here last week. I reckon Robson is still feeling the effects of that foul.'

'Anyway, it got us a goal.'

Gently pushed his way past them grimly, intent now only on getting out. He hadn't found it. He was going away empty-handed. And he had been so sure, so completely positive . . .! His whole instinct, buoyed on the pattern of the case, had told him that the trail would end that afternoon at Railway Road.

He felt, as Hansom had phrased it, like a kid who'd got his sums wrong. And it was a bitter pill for Gently to swallow. Yesterday, the thing had begun to move, it was on its way. It had only needed one more stroke . . . this one, and every nerve in his body had told him that he would find it that afternoon at Railway Road. But he'd been wrong, and he hadn't found it . . . the instinct that had carried him through so many cases had failed him.

Despairingly he thrust his way through the tight-packed crowd, looking at no one, caring for no one. He couldn't quite believe it had happened to him. Always before the luck that smiles on good detectives had smiled on him at the crucial moment . . . he felt suddenly that he must be getting old and past it. He was falling down on a case.

At the city end of Queen Street was a small, cheap café, nearly on the corner of Prince's Street. Gently went in, bought himself a cup of tea and some rolls, then sat down with them at a marble-topped table. He'd got to get himself straightened out, to get his thoughts in order. At the moment they were tumbling over each other in a wild commotion, refusing to come together in a coherent picture: while through them all wound the insidious echo – it was there, if you could have found it.

He bit the end off a roll that wasn't fresh and washed it down with some over-brewed tea. His mind was balking, it wouldn't settle down. Stupidly he began to fight his way back into the afternoon, beginning with his walk down Queen Street and adding to it, piece by piece, the people who went in front, the people who went behind, the cars that hooted, the programme-sellers using a sand-hopper for a stall. There was the bridge and the bridge-keeper, who wouldn't have noticed his own brother going by, and the bedlam of the car park with its entrance almost flush opposite the artery of Riverside.

Slowly the picture came into focus, the turnstile, the crowd running loose round the backs, the shove down into the terraces, the music of the loud-speakers. And the game with its end-of-the-season looseness, and the comments of the crowd round about. It came back now, sharp and incisive, even tiny details like the worn paint and patches of rust on the crush-rail. Gently munched on down the roll, the distant look came back into his eye. What had they said about the goalkeeper? Ken was standing in the goal and laughing at them. Well, he looked as though he might have been, up there, watching his team-mates make one glaring miss after another – 'Lord knows how Noel missed that last one.' But the championship was virtually settled: it was time to laugh at one's mistakes. 'At least it was a clean game . . . not like the lot last week.' That was true, there had been very few fouls. 'I reckon Robson is still feeling the effects of that foul.' 'Anyway, it got us a goal.'

Gently paused, the tail-end of the roll halfway between his plate and his mouth. The words echoed back through his mind: Robson . . . foul . . . goal. What was it there that struck a chord, that reached out towards some mental pigeon-hole with a faint, but definite persistence? He took a deep breath and put down the end of the roll. 'Have you got a phone I can use?' he asked the woman who was serving.

'You can use the one in the hall,' she replied, reluctantly.

Gently dialled and waited impatiently. 'Chief Inspector Gently . . . Is the super there?' They put him through to the super's office, but it was Hansom who answered the phone. Gently said: 'Look, Hansom, are the reports of those interrogations where you can lay hands on them?' Hansom snorted down the phone. 'Haven't you turned that job in yet . . .?' Gently said: 'This is important. I want you to read me over the first few questions and answers of the report on Leaming.'

There was a long pause while the phone recorded nothing but vague noises and shifts of sound. Then came the sound of Hansom picking up the instrument again. 'I've got the report here,' he said. 'What do you want to know?'

'Just start reading it.'

'It starts with some junk about football.'

'That's what I'm after . . . don't miss out a word.'

Hansom read in a sing-song voice: 'Chief Inspector Gently you'll be able to tell me who got the City's first goal yesterday was it Robson. Leaming it was Smethick actually he scored from a free kick after a foul on Jones S. Chief Inspector Gently ah yes in the twenty-second—'

'Wait!' interrupted Gently, 'let's have that bit again.'

'What – all of it?'

'The Leaming bit.'

Hansom repeated: Leaming it was Smethick actually he scored from a free kick after a foul on Jones S.'

'Ah!' murmured Gently, 'Jones S.!'

There came an impatient rustle from the other end. 'Say!' bawled Hansom, 'what the hell is this?'

Gently smiled cherubically. 'Never mind now . . . just keep that record where it won't get lost. Oh, and Hansom—'

'I'm still connected.'

'You might get on to the super and warn him that things could get exciting later on.'

'How do you mean – exciting?'

'Oh . . . you know . . . just exciting.' Gently pressed the instrument firmly down in its cradle, then lifted it and dialled again. 'Press office? I want the sports editor . . . no, I don't care if he is busy getting out the football – this is the police.' There was a short, busy pause, then a brisk hand seized the other instrument. 'Sports editor – who's that?'

'Chief Inspector Gently. I want some information about the report printed last week of the match at Railway Road.'

'Well . . . what is it?'

'Your account said that the City's first goal was scored by Smethick after a foul on Jones S., whereas I understand that the foul was on Robson. Can you corroborate that?'

'Yes – it was on Robson. Our reporter misread his notes when he was telephoning . . . we have to work at considerable speed to make the deadline.'

'That's all right,' said Gently genially, 'there's no need to apologize. A slip like that won't worry many people.'

CHAPTER SIXTEEN

L EAMING'S CAR STOOD stood in the corner of the timber-yard, a crouched glowing presence in the gathering dusk. One of the sliding doors of the machine shop stood ajar, sufficient to show a gleam of light in the office at the far end, and Gently, who was long-sighted, could make out the dark figure of the manager bent over his desk. Gently was in no hurry. He ambled over to the car and examined the doors, which were locked. Then he quietly raised the bonnet and removed a small item from the engine.

Leaming was so intent on his work that he failed to notice Gently's approach until warned by the creak of an opening door. But then he spun round and to his feet in one crisp movement. 'You!' he exclaimed, his dark eyes sharp and thrusting, 'what do you want?'

Gently shrugged and closed the glass-panelled door behind him. 'I've been to the football match,' he said, 'I thought you might like to hear about it.' He moved round from the door to Leaming's desk and peered disinterestedly at the open ledger. Leaming watched him closely. Gently felt in his pocket and produced two

237

peppermint creams, which he placed on the desk, pushing one towards Leaming with a stubby finger. 'Have one,' he said.

Leaming remained tense, watching.

Gently pulled up a little chair and sat down weightily. 'It wasn't a very good match. It was a bit end-of-the-season. And the *people*! I think it must have been near the ground record . . . forty-two thousand, isn't it?' His green eyes rose questioningly.

'A little more than that.'

'A little more?' Gently looked disappointed. 'I thought you would have been able to give me the exact figure . . . I know how precise you are about football matters.'

Leaming bit his lip. 'What does it matter, anyhow?'

'Oh, it doesn't, not really . . . but I thought you would have known.'

'It's forty-three thousand one hundred and twenty-one.'

'Ah!' Gently beamed at him. 'I was sure you could tell me. And wasn't that at the cup-tie with Pompey a couple of seasons ago . . . when Pompey won two-nought?'

Leaming came a step forward. 'See here,' he snapped, 'I don't know what you're after, and I don't care. But I've got work to do . . . we've got the accountants coming on Monday.'

'And you've got the "Straight Grain" books to prepare and make plausible before then . . . haven't you?'

Leaming seized the ledger on the desk, jerked it round and shoved it across to Gently. 'There!' he jeered. 'Have a look at it – see what you can find out.'

Gently shook his head. 'It isn't my job. We'll get a fraud man down to go through it.'

'A fraud man? Who's charging me with fraud?'

'Nobody . . . and as a matter of fact, I don't think anybody will.'

'Then what's this talk of getting a fraud man down?'

Gently continued to shake his head, slowly, woodenly. 'They'll want to know all about it in court, you know . . . the prosecution for the Crown will go into it with great thoroughness.'

There was a dead silence. Leaming stood immobile, his handsome face drained of all colour. Against the unnatural paleness his dark eyes seemed larger, darker, more penetrating than ever. 'What do you mean by that?' he asked huskily.

Gently turned away and said, speaking quickly: 'I've got the last piece of evidence I needed against you. There was a mistake in the account of the match which appeared in the *Football News* last Saturday. The same mistake appears in an answer you gave to one of my questions on Sunday . . . a record of it is in the files at police headquarters.'

'You found that out . . . today?'

'A short time ago. I overheard a scrap of conversation at the match this afternoon which led me to check with the Press office. I also checked your account in the police files.'

Leaming went back a pace, his hands grasping involuntarily. 'You're not lying?' he demanded suddenly.

'No, I'm not lying . . . why should I?'

'Suppose I said I wasn't at the match, but I was somewhere else?'

'No.' Gently shook his head again. 'It won't do. You'd have to prove it . . . and you can't prove it.'

'But you can't base a murder charge on that alone!'

Gently reached out for his peppermint cream, slow and deliberate. 'I can show that you had the motive,' he said. 'I can show that you could have hidden in the summer-house while Peter and his father were quarrelling. I can show that Fisher was watching what took place. I can show that Fisher blackmailed you first for Susan and then for the money. I can show that Fisher was murdered and he was murdered just when I had got sufficient evidence to make him speak – which you had grounds to suspect. I can show points of similarity between the two murders. I can show that you can prove no alibi at the time of Fisher's murder. I can show you were seen at the scene of the crime carrying a bag which subsequently became blood-stained and was destroyed here, where it is logical to suppose you would destroy it. I can show that the key which locked the door of Fisher's flat after the murder was found with it. And finally, I can now show that the alibi you gave for the time of the Huysmann murder was deliberately fabricated and completely false.'

'It's not enough – I'll get a defence to tear it to tatters!'

Gently bit into the peppermint cream. 'You might have done before today,' he said smoothly.

'It can't make all that difference . . . I won't believe it!'

'It was the one thing necessary.'

Leaming came forward again and leaned on the desk with both hands. 'Listen, Gently, listen – you can't go through with this. I'm talking to you now as a man, not as a police officer. All right, I admit it – I killed them both, Huysmann and Fisher, and you'll say I should be punished for it. But think a minute – there's a difference! Huysmann died, never knowing what had happened, and so did Fisher, instantaneously. They were both killed in hot blood, Gently. They were killed in the way of life, by their enemy, one man killing another to survive, Huysmann a vicious old man, Fisher a rat who asked for what he got. But you are after something different with me. If you go through with this, I shan't be killed that way. I'll be taken in cold blood, taken bound, taken with every man's hand against me, not a fight, not a chance, just taken and slaughtered in that death-pit of yours. That's the difference – that's what it amounts to! And I say to you as a man that you can't do it. You wouldn't match a killing of that sort with a killing of my sort, and clear your conscience by calling it justice!'

Gently stirred uneasily in his chair. 'I didn't make the laws – you knew the penalty that went with killing.'

'But it only goes with killing when a man's convicted – and I'm not convicted, and except for you I never would be!'

'I'm sorry, Leaming . . . it doesn't rest with me.'

'But it does rest with you – the local police are satisfied to let it go at the inquest verdict. They must know what you know . . . you work together. And they're satisfied, so why aren't you?'

'They don't know I've broken your alibi yet.'

'But they know the rest – and they're doing nothing about it.'

Gently turned away from him, his face looking tired. 'It's no good, Leaming . . . I've got to do it. When a man begins to kill it gets easier and easier for him, and it has to be stopped. I'm the person whose duty it is to stop him. And I've got to stop you.'

'Even if you have to deliver me to a state killing party?'

'I'm a policeman, not a lawgiver.'

'But you're a man as well!'

'Not while I'm a policeman . . . we're not permitted to have thoughts like that. The law allows me only one way to stop killing . . . it's not my way, but it's the only way.'

'Then you're going through with it?'

'Yes, I'm going through with it.'

Leaming drew back from the desk, as far as the closed door. 'Then you leave me no option but to kill you too, Gently,' he said.

Gently looked up at him with unmoved green eyes. 'I realized it would come to that, of course . . . but it won't be easy for you.'

Leaming felt casually in his pocket and produced a small automatic. 'It will be as easy as this,' he said. The colour had come back into his cheeks now and something of the old jauntiness to his manner. 'I'm sorry it's come to this, Gently. I didn't want to do any more killing . . . whatever you may think about killing getting easier, I assure you it's something one would rather not do. And I don't want to kill you, because I admire you. But I have a duty to myself, just as you have a duty to the state.'

Gently said: 'It won't help you to kill me. They'll come straight to you for it.'

Leaming said: 'But they won't find anything . . . and I don't care what they suspect. I shall tip your body into the incinerator at Hellston Tofts and the gun after you. It isn't traceable . . . I bought it on the black market.'

'What about the noise of the shot?'

Leaming smiled frostily. 'Nobody's going to hear that. I shall shoot you here, in the shop.'

'But it's perfectly quiet?'

'It won't be when I shoot you. I shall have all the saws running – the people round here are used to hearing that. We sometimes run them after hours for test purposes.'

Gently reached out for the second peppermint cream. 'When I'm missing they'll come straight to you,' he repeated. 'Hansom knows there's something vital in that answer of yours in the records. He doesn't know what it is, but he'll find out, and the fact that I'm missing will clinch the case for him. Suppose you stop killing and start thinking about your defence?'

Leaming shook his head briefly. 'I'll risk that,' he said, 'now come along with me while I switch the saws on.' He made a movement with his gun.

Gently hung on, mechanically chewing at the peppermint cream. If he refused to go, Leaming was faced with the prospect of shooting him where he sat and thus rousing the neighbourhood. But the rousing of the neighbourhood would be ill-appreciated by a dead Gently. He got up and shambled over to the door.

Leaming switched on the lights as they passed them, flooding the huge, wide sheds with fluorescent glare. He kept Gently walking three paces ahead. The first of the saws broke into life with a snatching whirr, quickly rising, becoming a loud, shuddering drone. Leaming said: 'We must find one with a piece of timber in the feed . . . if I put that through at the appropriate moment I should be all right.' Saw by saw they worked round the shop. The still air became virulent with the high, pulsating drone, throbbing and writhing in waves of vicious power, naked and potential. It made Gently feel sick. It was as though a vast, anti-human power were building up, as though it were rising towards a peak at which his organism would disintegrate, would tear apart, smashed into its component atoms. Leaming set off some band-saws. Their whining shriek imposed itself on the roar of the circulars like a theme of madness twisting through chaos, a sharp, demonic ecstasy of destruction. 'How's that?' bawled Leaming. 'Do you think they'll hear a shot through this lot?' Gently said nothing, would not look back at him.

They went to the centre saws now, moving back towards the sliding doors. Near the further end was a little wooden booth, perhaps for a time-keeper, glass-panelled at the top. Gently kept his eye on it. Slowly they drew closer, moving between pauses while Leaming set going the saws at each side. They drew abreast of it, Leaming going first to the saw on his left, then stepping across to the one on his right.

The noise in the shop was so deafening that the crash of the falling booth was scarcely audible. But Gently heard the riposte of the gun. He didn't stay to argue. A second shot followed the first like an echo and a whiff of white dust sprang up at his feet. He leaped sideways, bending low to get cover from the saws, and made towards the gaping doorway. But Leaming had anticipated the move and sprinted like the wind to cut him off. A bullet out of nowhere warned Gently that he wouldn't get out of the doors.

Zig-zagging, still keeping cover behind the saws, Gently worked back towards the office and the switch-board. If he could put the lights out for a moment . . . But once again Leaming sensed his objective and rushed to cut him off. A fourth bullet smacked into a baulk of wood a couple of feet away. He dodged away behind the tearing saws.

He was getting cornered now, driven back towards the band-saws. Up there it was a dead-end, no door, no windows, and the band-saws didn't give cover like the circulars did. Desperately he tried to double out of the trap, but the agile Leaming beat him each time. He wasn't shooting now at every glimpse – he was holding his last two bullets. And slowly, almost leisurely, he was herding Gently towards the dead-end, where the outcome was inevitable.

With the scream of the band-saws ripping at his ear-drums Gently hung on behind the last circular. Leaming was coming across diagonally towards it, gun low, stooping, like a predatory animal moving in to the kill. Gently saw him past the rippling steel blade, intent, remorseless, moving in. He also saw something else. It was a jack-wrench lying on the saw-bench. His clumsy hand rose up over the edge of the bench and fastened on the handle. On came Leaming, aware of his presence, gun at the ready now. Gently crouched further back along the saw. He saw the face loom up with the look of the kill in its dark eyes, the arm move from the shoulder to fire over the saw-bench ... then he hurled the jack-wrench squarely into the thundering circle of burnished steel.

Flat on the floor, he never knew quite what happened after that. His next coherent impression was of a sudden slackening of the fearful noise, a dying away, combined with complete darkness and the sickening smell of burned-out cable. Trembling, he got to his feet and fumbled for his lighter. Its tiny flame snapped dazzlingly before his eyes. The first thing he saw was Leaming's gun, lying quite close to him. Instinctively he checked a movement to grab it, pulled out his handkerchief, picked up the gun by the end of its still-warm muzzle.

With ears buzzing he picked his way towards the office and the phone. He put out his lighter and dialled by touch. 'Super there? Put me through to him . . . Chief Inspector Gently.' There was practically no pause at all before the super's voice came on with a barrage of questions. Gently covered the receiver wearily. 'Listen,' he said. There was a silence and presumably the super was listening. 'I'm in the office of Huysmann's yard. I'd like you to come along now for a bit of routine work . . . you'll need an ambulance amongst other things, and bring plenty of torches because I've wrecked the electrics hereabouts . . .' He paused and held the instrument away from him while the super reacted. 'Yes, I have got Leaming here . . . I broke his alibi and he confessed . . . then he pulled a gun and took a few shots at me, but he isn't all that good at shooting . . . he's a bit off-colour just now, though he should be in shape for a trial by the autumn.'

Gently clamped down the receiver and sat quite still for a moment or two. His ears still buzzed with the pounding they had taken, his hands were still trembling and he felt unutterably tired. Outside in the shop a great silence prevailed, a thick, dark silence, like the inside of the pyramids. Somewhere on the surface of it he could hear a car passing down Queen Street, very distant, a sound from another world. And then came the far-away clamour of a bell which was the ambulance, probably as it shot the lights at Grove Lane.

CHAPTER SEVENTEEN

THERE WASN'T A lot to be made out of the news that the manager of Huysmann's had been injured at the yard and taken to hospital, even though the police did wait at his bedside until he regained consciousness. The Norchester Press, for instance, was very restrained and non-committal. But the Norchester Press was like that anyway. It didn't deceive Charlie for one moment. Charlie knew, if nobody else did, that Chief Inspector Gently had been 'after' Leaming. Hadn't he seen Gently there, with his own eyes, playing with Leaming just as, formerly, he had played with Fisher? Then it was Leaming after all who'd knocked the old man off . . . a man like Gently wasn't going to be fooled by Fisher cutting his throat. Charlie's only anxiety was that Leaming wouldn't pull round. Unless there was a trial, nobody would really know how right Charlie had been.

But he needn't have worried. They took good care of Leaming at the Norchester and County Hospital and lavished a small fortune of drugs and surgical talent on him. A man must look his best when he's likely to be hung . . . also, the trial that followed was magnificent, even by Charlie's standards.

Peter Huysmann returned home to take over the management of the yard himself, bringing with him his wife and the good wishes of the fair community. Cathy was a little nervous of Gretchen, but Gretchen was only too pleased to have a companion to liven up the gloom of the Huysmann house. Mrs Turner improved the occasion by reading a homily to Susan on taking up with men, especially the managerial classes. It fell a little flat. Susan had already ceased to mourn the loss of Leaming and was viewing with interest the attentions of the brewery executive from up the road.

Hansom's generosity was rather strained when it came to congratulating Gently a second time. In his private opinion, Gently was an exponent of art for art's sake. There had been no need to take things further than Fisher . . . they had ended there very neatly. If Fisher wasn't exactly responsible for Huysmann's death, he was as near to it as made no difference, and to go on after that was untidy and a little precious . . . especially with so little in the way of evidence. But he was a nice type really, was Hansom. At parting, he gave Gently one of his best cigars.

The super said snappishly: 'I can't think why the devil you went after him alone, when you might have taken the entire City Police with you. Surely you realized he might be tempted to add you to his other victims?'

Gently shook his head in his wooden way. 'I had to give him enough rope. If we'd simply pulled him in he'd still have had a pretty good case to argue . . . he had to be made to do something silly. Of course, I didn't know he'd got a gun.'

'Oh! So you didn't know he'd got a gun! And would it have made any difference if you had known?'

'No . . . not really.'

'Well, it would have done to me – I can tell you that!' The super sniffed in an aggrieved sort of way. 'I've given up trying to understand you people,' he said. 'As far as I can see, you're either born to homicide or you aren't, and if you aren't, you might just as well keep your big mouth shut and pretend your corpses aren't there. When did you start suspecting Leaming?'

Gently applied a light to his waning pipe. 'I didn't suspect anyone. I just kept finding things out till I'd got a pattern.'

'And why didn't the pattern fit Fisher?'

'Oh . . . I don't know. He wasn't clever enough. If he'd done murder and stolen forty thousand he'd have run off with it, not hung around.'

'And Peter Huysmann?'

'I saw him riding the Wall of Death . . . I knew he hadn't done it.'

'How about the girl Gretchen – and the maid?'

'Gretchen wasn't strong enough to strike the blow that killed Huysmann, and as for the maid—!' Gently smiled lazily. 'I had my fun, too . . . I took Susan to the pictures one night.'

The super's eyes glinted. 'That wasn't professional of you, Gently!'

Gently sighed, and knocked out his pipe.

There were two yachtsmen on the river that summer who were very keen photographers. They took photographs of almost everything that came their way. One of these photographs won first prize in the Norchester Press Summer Snaps Competition and was duly published on the front page, right opposite a screed about the manager of a timber-yard being charged with double murder. It was entitled 'Tomorrow *may* be Friday' and depicted a bulky individual sitting asleep on the river-bank, his fishing-rod trailing in the water, his hands clasped on his stomach and a bag of sweets open beside him.

Inspector Hansom saw this photograph. He bought three copies of it and pinned one up on the cupboard door at his office. It kept him happy for weeks.